# THE TEXAS TATTLER

***All The News You Need To Know...And More!***

Maybe it's just us, but a certain Texas Cattleman's Club member sure has been spending an awful lot of time at the new Helping Hands Women's Shelter. At first, it seemed as if this mega-rich rancher was just being neighborly and philanthropic. But we've caught a glimpse of the shelter's newest advocate. There's no way that TCC member has not noticed as well. He is, after all, a red-blooded Texan!

But what about this new girl in town? She certainly couldn't have missed that tall, dark and handsome rancher hanging around. And we all know how many women have been throwing themselves at this certain bachelor for his lovely loot. (Money and looks? Sign us up!) Has she been helping out at Helping Hands purely for compassionate reasons…or to get *her* hands on a millionaire?

Dear Reader,

I feel honored to again participate in a TEXAS CATTLEMAN'S CLUB continuity.

I love Texan men, which is why my hero from my very first book was from Texas. My fondest memories as a little girl were sharing the couch with my dad while watching some of the great westerns such as *Rawhide, Gunsmoke, Bonanza, Maverick* and so many others. All the leading men in those series were true heroes of the Wild West. The men of the TEXAS CATTLEMAN'S CLUB are the same type of heroes.

I enjoyed writing Darius and Summer's story as they realized what they had was love in the truest form, but it took a dosage of faith and trust to make it stronger. Both had been hurt by love but were willing to give it another try.

I want to thank all the other five authors who are a part of this continuity. I enjoyed working with each of you.

Happy reading!

*Brenda Jackson*

BRENDA JACKSON

# ONE NIGHT WITH THE WEALTHY RANCHER

Silhouette® Desire

Published by Silhouette Books

**America's Publisher of Contemporary Romance**

Recycling programs for this product may not exist in your area.

ISBN-13: 978-0-373-76958-2

ONE NIGHT WITH THE WEALTHY RANCHER



This edition published by arrangement with Harlequin Books S.A.



Visit Silhouette Books at www.eHarlequin.com

**Printed in U.S.A.**

**Books by Brenda Jackson**

Silhouette Desire

*Delaney's Desert Sheikh* #1473
*A Little Dare* #1533
*Thorn's Challenge* #1552
*Scandal Between the Sheets* #1573
*Stone Cold Surrender* #1601
*Riding the Storm* #1625
*Jared's Counterfeit Fiancée* #1654
*Strictly Confidential Attraction* #1677
*The Chase Is On* #1690
*Taking Care of Business* #1705
*The Durango Affair* #1727
*Ian's Ultimate Gamble* #1756
*Seduction, Westmoreland Style* #1778
*Stranded with the Tempting Stranger* #1825
*Spencer's Forbidden Passion* #1838
*Taming Clint Westmoreland* #1850
*Cole's Red-Hot Pursuit* #1874
*Quade's Babies* #1911
*Tall, Dark...Westmoreland!* #1928
*One Night with the Wealthy Rancher* #1958

*The Westmorelands

---

## *BRENDA JACKSON*

is a die "heart" romantic who married her childhood sweetheart and still proudly wears the "going steady" ring he gave her when she was fifteen. Because she's always believed in the power of love, Brenda's stories all have happy endings. In her real-life love story, Brenda and her husband of thirty-six years live in Jacksonville, Florida, and have two sons.

A *New York Times* bestselling author of more than fifty romance titles, Brenda is a recent retiree who worked thirty-seven years in management at a major insurance company. She divides her time between family, writing and traveling with Gerald. You may write Brenda at P.O. Box 28267, Jacksonville, Florida 32226, by e-mail at WriterBJackson@aol.com, or visit her Web site at www.brendajackson.net.

Special thanks and acknowledgment to Brenda Jackson
for her contribution to the Texas Cattleman's Club:
Maverick County Millionaires miniseries.

To the love of my life, Gerald Jackson, Sr.

To everyone who joined me on the
Madaris/Westmoreland Family Reunion 2009
Cruise to Canada. This one is for you!

"Provide things honest in the sight of all men."
—*Romans* 12:17

## Texas Cattleman's Club

#1952 *Taming the Texas Tycoon*—
Katherine Garbera, July 2009

#1958 *One Night with the Wealthy Rancher*—
Brenda Jackson, August 2009

#1964 *Texan's Wedding-Night Wager*—
Charlene Sands, September 2009

#1970 *The Oilman's Baby Bargain*—
Michelle Celmer, October 2009

#1977 *The Maverick's Virgin Mistress*—
Jennifer Lewis, November 2009

#1983 *Lone Star Seduction*—
Day Leclaire, December 2009

# One

"What are you doing here, Summer?"

Summer Martindale's eyes froze on the document in front of her at the sound of the husky voice. It was a voice she hadn't heard in almost seven years, yet she distinctively remembered the sensuous timbre and how every audible vibration could stir her senses in a way that even today she could not explain.

In a way she wished she could forget.

She inhaled deeply and after a moment, she lifted her eyes and stared into Darius Franklin's dark and intense gaze. It was a gaze that was emitting a chilling glare.

Summer could just as easily glare back but refused to let him know how disturbing it was to see him again. What had once been between them was over and done with. He had made sure of that in the worst possible way, which she could never forgive him for. His actions had caused her pain—a degree of pain she vowed never to experience again.

"I could ask you the same thing, Darius," she finally responded. Her tone was just as sharp as his had been.

He stood tall, all six foot one inches of him, as he leaned in the doorway with his arms crossed over his chest and his gaze fixed directly on her. She thought at that moment the very same thing she'd thought when she'd first laid eyes on him. Darius Franklin, with his pecan tan complexion, close-cut black hair, charcoal gray eyes and neat pencil-thin mustache, was an extremely handsome man. But there were other noticeable changes. His cheekbones appeared more pronounced and his lips seemed firmer.

His dark stare, as well as the way a muscle seemed to twitch in his jaw, were all the evidence she needed that he wasn't happy to see her and if truth be told, she wasn't happy to see him, either. It would be a lie to claim she hadn't thought about him over the years, because she had. Yet at the same time, the memory of what he'd put her through—the humiliation, heartbreak and pain—made her regret ever lowering her guard and letting him into her life.

He stepped away from the door and she watched his every move, wishing she weren't drawn to how fit his body was, and wishing a tug of desire had not invaded her stomach. Although he wasn't as lean as he used to be, he wore his masculinity well. Well-toned muscles outlined his chest and shoulders—muscles she could easily see through the material of his chambray shirt. And then there were jeans that hugged his firm hips and strong thighs. They were thighs that could keep a tight hold on hers as he thrust deeper and deeper inside of her.

She forced the turbulent memories away. Her gaze moved back up to his eyes and she tried not to flinch at the cold look in them. Something inside her shivered and she wondered how a man she had once fallen in love with so deeply could end up treating her so shabbily.

"I live here in Somerset."

His voice cut through Summer's thoughts. *He lived here in Somerset? Maverick County?* That information immediately filled her with apprehension and dread, as well as curiosity. *When had he left the Houston Police Department and why?*

"I live in Somerset, as well," she heard herself say. "I moved to town last month to work here at Helping Hands as a social worker."

Surprise lit his eyes. "A social worker?"

"Yes."

She understood his surprise. When he'd last seen her seven years ago, he'd been twenty-four years old and a detective with the Houston Police Department. And she'd been a nineteen-year-old trying to escape the clutches of an abusive fiancé by the name of Tyrone Whitman. After she had broken off their engagement, Tyrone had refused to get out of her life, to leave her alone. He had stalked her for months before he'd finally caught her alone in her apartment, and for three hours he had held a gun to her head, threatening to blow her brains out.

While the SWAT team had been trying to talk Tyrone into surrendering, Darius had broken into the apartment by coming through a bathroom window. He'd apprehended Tyrone and saved her. That night, Darius Franklin had become her knight in shining armor.

He was the same man who had stopped by her apartment the next day to repair the window, and the same man who, after learning that a not-too-smart judge had posted bail for Tyrone, made it his business to become her protector until the trial. After that, he was the same man who she began seeing on a daily basis, who would drop by when his shift changed to spend time with her, to show her how special he thought she was.

The same man who during that time, for one night, had been her lover.

"So, you went to college and got your degree?" he asked, and for a split second she could have sworn she detected a degree of admiration in his voice, but the look in his hard gaze told her she'd been wrong.

"Yes, I got my degree," she responded, proud of her accomplishment and quickly remembering he was one of the few people who'd encouraged her to do so, and convinced her that she could. He had made her believe in herself. And a part of her had believed in them, in a future together. He had proven her wrong.

"Congratulations."

"Thank you," she said briskly, putting aside the document she had been reading. "So, why are you here, Darius? Although we've established the fact that we're both living in Somerset, I'm sure this town is big enough for the both of us. What brings you to Helping Hands?"

"I'm here to install the security system as well as the billing account for the shelter," he said, as if that explained everything.

She nodded. "I was told the Texas Cattleman's Club would be sending someone over to do those things," she said, finding it hard to concentrate.

She had heard a lot about the Texas Cattleman's Club, a group of men who considered themselves the protectors of Texas and whose members consisted of the wealthiest men in Texas, mostly from old money. The TCC was known to help a number of worthy causes in the community and Helping Hands, a newly opened women's shelter located in the small, impoverished section of wealthy Maverick County, was one of them. They provided all the shelter's funding.

Summer had interviewed for the position at the shelter and once she had been offered the job, had decided it would be a good way to have a fresh start. She had made the move from Austin, where she had been living for the past six years.

"How did you get the job?" She couldn't help but ask.

He shrugged. "I own a security company."

She raised a brow, surprised he had gotten out of law enforcement. He'd made a good police detective and she'd figured it would be his career. "How long have you been living in Somerset?" she asked.

"Around six years."

It was the same amount of time she had lived in Austin. He had moved here a year after they had broken up. She quickly recalled that they really hadn't broken up since they had never truly been together…at least not like she'd assumed they had.

"If you're through with your interrogation, I'd like to get to work," he said.

"Fine. I'll get out of your way if you need to work in here for a while," she said, getting up from her desk. Seeing him again after all this time was just a bit too much. Bittersweet memories were trying to invade her brain and she was determined to fight them back.

"If you need anything, just let the shelter's secretary, Marcy Dillard, know. I'll use this time to go to lunch."

She grabbed her purse out of her desk drawer and quickly moved past him toward the door.

"Summer?"

She paused just before reaching the door and turned around. "Yes?"

He still had a hard look in his eyes. "I would say welcome to town, but I wouldn't mean it."

She narrowed her gaze. "Then I guess that means we'll have to learn to tolerate each other, doesn't it?"

Without waiting for him to respond, she turned and continued walking out the door.

* * *

Darius leaned back against the desk and watched Summer until she was no longer in sight. It was only then that he made an attempt to begin breathing normally again. But it was hard because although he couldn't see her, he still managed to feel her presence.

Seven years was a long time, yet today when a startled Summer had looked up at him and met his gaze, he'd felt a sensation that was like a swift kick in the gut. Potent memories had flooded his mind, forcing him to recall what she had come to mean to him in such a short period of time, and just how deep her betrayal had cut.

He hit his fist on the desk, angry and frustrated. How could he still find her so desirable after all this time? After all she'd done? Why had seeing her sent sensuous shivers down his spine? She was seven years older, no longer a mere nineteen-year-old who hadn't decided what she wanted out of life other than to be free of an obsessive ex-fiancé. She was just as stunning as he remembered. Even more so.

She had matured beautifully. She was about five-eight, tall and slim with shoulder-length straight brown hair and hazel eyes he could always drown in. Her skin tone, the color of café au lait, had always tempted him to lick her all over.

Darius bowed his head momentarily as even more memories he had tried so hard to forget resurfaced.

After college, he'd gotten a job with the Houston Police Department as a detective with aspirations of moving up the ranks. Authorities had been called to the scene regarding a domestic dispute, and Darius and his partner, Walt Stewart, had been the first to arrive.

A young woman who had obtained a restraining order against her ex-fiancé was in danger. The man, named Tyrone Whitman, had broken into her apartment and was holding a gun to her head, threatening to kill her unless she took him back.

While Walt tried talking him into surrendering, Darius was able to get into the apartment through a rear bathroom window, overtake Whitman and free Summer.

Concern for her safety when Whitman was released on bond allowed Darius to convince himself that it was important to keep checking on her. But then it became obvious it was a lot more than that. Point-blank, he had been attracted to her and thought she was a special woman who'd gotten mixed up with the wrong guy, and was trying to get her life together. Against his better judgment, although he'd been warned by Walt that Summer wasn't really what she seemed, he had fallen for her, and fallen hard.

He'd assumed he had gotten to know her, and thought she felt the same way after a night they had spent together filled with so much sexual chemistry that it could only end one way: they had made love. Deep, passionate love. Shudders passed through him just remembering that night and the effect it had on him. It was a night he could never forget, although over the past seven years he had tried like hell to do so.

*And it was a night that apparently had meant more to him than it had to her.*

The following day he had left town when he received word of his brother Ethan's near-fatal car accident. He'd had to leave immediately for Charleston and when he couldn't reach Summer, and had been unable to leave her a message because her voice-mail box was full, he'd left word with his partner to let her know what happened. When he had returned to Houston a week later, he discovered that Summer had packed up and left town without leaving word as to where she'd gone. She'd told Walt to tell him that she wanted to build a new life for herself and was leaving town with an older man. A very wealthy one—something Darius was not.

After nearly losing his brother, it had almost destroyed him to find out that he had lost her, that she had turned her back on what could have been between them to take up with a man with money.

A hard smile formed on his lips and he wondered what she would think to discover that he was now a wealthy man, thanks to smart investments and the success of his security firm. She thought he'd been hired as a laborer for the TCC—he could just imagine her reaction when she discovered he was a member of the Texas Cattleman's Club. The same club that was funding the shelter, including her salary.

Another thought crept into his mind, one that made his skin crawl. What if she knew already? What if the reason she was in Somerset was because she'd heard about his success and assumed after all this time she could ease her way back in his good graces? A woman looking for a wealthy husband would do just about anything. He'd been gullible before and wondered if she thought he would be gullible again. Considering her actions seven years ago, he wouldn't put anything past her.

He leaned against her desk as those thoughts filled his mind. She wasn't wearing a ring on her finger, which was a good indication that she wasn't married. And she *had* acted surprised to see him. But then it could have very well been an act. He had found out the hard way just what a good actress she was. One thing was for certain: he wouldn't be letting his guard down. She had taken advantage of his heart before but she wouldn't be doing so again.

He was about to begin the work he'd come to do when his cell phone went off. Recognizing the special ringtone, he pulled it off his belt and clicked it on. "Yes, Lance?"

"Hey, man, sorry I missed your call earlier."

"No problem. I just wanted you to know that I heard from Fire Chief Ingle. I'm meeting with him tomorrow evening to go over some things. He indicated that he'll have the official report ready in a week and that it contains proof that the fire was deliberately set."

Lance Brody was Darius's best friend from college at the University of Texas, where the two of them, along with another good friend, Kevin Novak, had been roommates. The three had forged a bond that would last a lifetime. There was nothing one wouldn't do for the other and Darius could rightly say that he could give his two friends credit for his financial success.

Lance, along with his younger brother Mitch, had come from old money and together they owned Brody Oil and Gas Company. The two had included Darius in a number of successful investment opportunities. So had Kevin, who'd made his fortune in real estate development.

Lance and Kevin had grown up in Somerset and had tried convincing Darius to move there after college but he had opted for the job in Houston instead. Then, shortly after that incident with Summer, he'd decided he would move to Somerset to start a new career and a new life.

He worked closely with his friends, and Lance had hired him to investigate a fire at the Brody Oil and Gas refinery a few weeks ago. Although there was significant damage, no one had gotten seriously hurt. Darius had no doubt the fire had been the work of an arsonist, and now Chief Ingle had confirmed his suspicions.

"I can't wait until we nail Alex. I intend to make sure that he rots in jail," Lance was saying.

Lance and Mitch were certain they knew the identity of the arsonist. He was the long-time hated rival of the Brodys, a man by the name of Alejandro "Alex" Montoya.

"Calm down, Lance. The man is innocent until proven guilty," Darius said.

"Wait until the report comes out. Mark my word, Alex Montoya is the person behind that fire."

"That may very well be the case," Darius said, knowing just how convinced Lance was of Alex's guilt. "But it has to be proven. How's Kate?" Darius asked, trying to change the subject. Lance and Kate had eloped to Vegas a few weeks ago.

"Kate's fine and I know what you're trying to do, Darius."

Darius couldn't help but chuckle. "If you know, then humor me. I need like hell to laugh about now."

"Sounds like it's been one of those days for you," Lance said.

"You don't know the half of it. Summer is here."

There was a pause. "Summer? *Your* Summer?"

Darius could have really laughed out loud at that one, since Summer had never truly been his. But at one time he'd thought she was, and he had told Lance all about her. "Yes, Summer Martindale."

"What's she doing in Somerset?"

Darius sighed deeply. "She's a social worker at Helping Hands. I showed up to set up security and work on the billing system for the place, and walked right into her office."

"Must have been one hell of a reunion."

"Hey, what can I say?"

Lance chuckled. "You can say you need a drink. Sounds like it, anyway. Meet me at the TCC Café when you're ready to take a break for lunch."

Moments later, Darius hung up the phone thinking Lance was right. He needed a drink.

Summer settled into the booth at the Red Sky Café three blocks from the shelter. It was the first week of

August and such a beautiful day that she had enjoyed the walk. It had given her a chance to compose herself after seeing Darius again.

She glanced around the café. The Red Sky was a place she had been frequenting for lunch since working at Helping Hands and she had become friendly with the owners. The Timmons had grown up in this section of Maverick County and had been instrumental in approaching members of the TCC about the need for a shelter in the community.

The shelter was a full-service center that provided a safe place for women who'd experienced all types of violence to heal and plan for their future. Helping Hands had opened their doors a few months ago and she'd been hired as part of its counseling team. Summer couldn't help but appreciate the members of the Texas Cattleman's Club for funding the shelter. She of all people knew how important such a facility was.

She had dated Tyrone for a few months, but it was only after they'd gotten engaged that she'd discovered his mean-spirited, possessive nature that on occasion would become abusive, both mentally and physically. She had sought the help of a shelter in Houston and there had found the strength to break things off with him. The social worker at the shelter had helped her to see that although she couldn't control Tyrone's behavior toward her, she could control how she responded to it and remove herself from the situation.

Her choice to end things was something Tyrone couldn't accept and he had begun stalking her, which was the reason she'd put the restraining order in place. Months had gone by when he'd appeared at her apartment one night, and forced his way inside, threatening her life. Chills went up her spine as she remembered that time.

After her own horrible experience with Tyrone, not to mention her heartbreak with Darius, she didn't trust her instincts where men were concerned so she just left them alone. Over the years she had buried herself in her books, getting her degree. After college she had concentrated on her work as an advocate for battered women.

"What are you going to have today, Miss Martindale?"

Summer smiled as she glanced up into the face of Tina Kay, one of the waitresses. Tina had been one of her first clients at Helping Hands and at seventeen, one of her youngest. A runaway after being shifted from foster home to foster home, Tina had become the victim of physical abuse at the hands of her boyfriend, a guy who had convinced her she deserved the beatings he'd been giving her.

Summer couldn't help but recall her own story. After high school, she had wanted to see the world. Aunt Joanne, who had raised her after her parents had been killed in a car accident when she was thirteen, tried to get her to remain in Birmingham. But she'd left Alabama to work her way to California. Along the way, she ended up in Houston where she found a job as a waitress at a chain restaurant. That's where she'd met Tyrone. The company he worked for frequently made deliveries to the restaurant. Something told her he was bad news, but she had wanted to believe there was some good in him. Boy, had she been wrong.

"Just the usual," Summer finally said, relaxing in her seat, looking forward to her grilled chicken salad.

She took a moment to study Tina, who looked so different than the young woman who'd come to the shelter with a swollen eye, cuts around her mouth and bruises on various parts of her body. "And how have you been doing, Tina?" she asked.

Tina's smile widened. "I've been doing fine. The Timmons are letting me use the apartment above their garage. I've enrolled to take classes at the local community college next month and thought I'd brush up on my math. That's always been my weakest subject. I ordered one of those do-it-yourself math books online."

"And how are those self-defense classes going?" The shelter offered the classes weekly and attendance was always at capacity.

"They've been great. The instructor is just awesome. I've learned a number of techniques to protect myself."

She could hear the excitement in Tina's voice and felt good about it. The man who had roughed Tina up had left town but there was a warrant out for his arrest. Summer's thoughts shifted to Tyrone, who'd gotten a twenty-year sentence. It would have been less if he hadn't told the judge just where he could shove it. She shook her head, wondering how she could have ever thought that she loved the man. She could now admit that at eighteen she had been young and rather foolish.

"I'll be back with your order in a second," Tina said.

When Tina walked off, Summer settled back in her seat, allowing herself to think about the man she'd left at the shelter. The one man she had tried so hard to forget. She'd thought moving to Somerset would be a fresh start. A new town. New people. A new job. She hadn't figured on being confronted with a blast from her past.

One thing she told the women she counseled at the shelter was that they could confront and conquer any challenge they were presented with, and she knew she needed to take that same advice. Fate was playing a cruel trick by putting her and Darius in the same town. But she would handle it. And she would handle him.

An irritated and frustrated Darius walked into the TCC Café and glanced around at his surroundings. What used to be a twenty-six-room mansion had been converted into a place where the TCC members could unwind and relax, which was just what he needed.

In addition to the café, the TCC also included a golf course, a state-of-the-art spa, riding stables and an air-conditioned pool house with a retractable roof as well as numerous meeting rooms, game rooms, a well-stocked library and a formal dining room.

Darius, Lance and Kevin, along with Mitch and

another friend of the Brodys named Justin Dupree, spent a lot of time shooting pool in the game room. Last fall they were practically glued to the club's projection television screen during football season.

He saw Lance sitting at a table in the back. The café served both lunch and dinner and it wasn't uncommon for Lance to meet him here for lunch. However, nowadays Lance was quick to rush back to the office since his new wife Kate had decided to remain at Brody Oil and Gas as Lance's administrative assistant.

Darius shook his head. Knowing Lance the way he did, he doubted his best friend let Kate get much work done. Hell, he wouldn't either if he had the woman he loved pretty much underfoot all day.

*The woman he loved.*

Something twisted in his gut at the thought. Thanks to Summer, he doubted he would ever be able to love another woman again.

"I need a beer," he said, frowning, sliding into the booth across from Lance.

"I've already ordered you one. I was looking out the window when you drove up," Lance said, studying Darius carefully.

"Thanks. I had hoped to at least get the security analysis completed on most of the computers today so I can decide what software will work best," Darius said, smiling a thanks to the waitress who placed a mug of beer in front of him.

"So, you're going to do it instead of one of your men?"

Darius nodded. "Heath left yesterday for Los

Angeles to guard some actress who's been getting death threats, and Milt is still in Dallas," he said of two of the six men who worked for him. "The others have been assigned to various other projects around town. That means I'll have to go back over to the shelter when I leave here."

Lance nodded as he took a plug from his own beer. "It also means you'll be seeing Summer again."

Darius didn't say anything. Yes, that meant he would probably see Summer again today. No telling how many more times he'd see her before he finished up what needed to be done at the shelter.

Because of the nature of what went on at women's shelters, Helping Hands needed top security twenty-four hours a day, seven days a week. The TCC had decided to upgrade all the computers to eliminate the risk of getting hacked. The majority of the women seeking refuge at the shelter were the victims of domestic violence, women whose lives could be placed in danger if their batterers discovered their whereabouts.

"Tell me about her, Darius."

Darius met Lance's gaze. "I've practically told you everything about how we met and how things ended. She went to college and got a degree, and now works for the shelter."

"Did you mention anything to her about being a member of TCC?"

"No. She thinks my company was hired to handle security at the shelter."

Lance smiled. “In a way, that’s true.”

“Yes, which is why she doesn’t need to know any different.” Darius felt his face harden when he said, “There can never be anything between me and Summer again.”

Yet he knew making sure of that wouldn’t be easy. Summer was the type of woman who easily got under a man’s skin. Just the memory of walking into that office and finding her sitting behind the desk had the power to make him feel weak and vulnerable.

And that was the one thing he could not let happen. He did not have a special woman in his life and preferred keeping it that way. Desire for anything more had died seven years ago with Summer’s betrayal.

# Two

"Mr. Franklin wanted me to let you know he left for lunch but will be coming back, Ms. Martindale."

"Oh. Thanks, Marcy," Summer said, trying to keep her voice as normal as she could. After taking a file off Marcy's top tray, she went into her office and closed the door behind her.

Today she had taken an extra-long lunch, hoping by the time she returned Darius would have finished what he'd come to do. But it seemed that would not be the case. Summer bit her lip, deciding she would be professional as well as mature about the matter. He had a job to do and so did she, and as long as they each knew where the other stood, there was no reason they couldn't at least be decent to each other. But then what right did he have to be upset with her since she was the injured party? He was the one who'd left town after discussing their night together with his partner. He probably didn't know Walt had told her the truth, and he was upset because she had left town when he'd returned. It was crazy how men thought sometimes, but it didn't matter now. He had made it quite clear what he thought of her and she hoped she'd left no doubt in his mind just what she thought of him. So there. That was that.

She dropped down in her chair thinking, no, that wasn't that at all. Not as long as the sight of him could send sensations oozing up her spine. Whenever he looked at her, even with anger flaring in the dark depths of his eyes, she felt stirrings in places she didn't want to think about. He'd always had that effect on her. In the past she'd welcomed it, but now she despised it.

She drew in a deep breath and for the first time in years, she felt like the world was closing in on her. It had taken her a while after leaving Houston to pull herself together and decide that no man—Tyrone or Darius—was worth that much pain. But she had moved on with her life. She was proud of her accomplishment and intended to obtain her doctorate after working in her field a few years.

"Don't you have anything to do?"

Summer blinked and saw Darius standing in her doorway. She glared at him—so much for thinking they could be decent to each other. "You should have knocked before entering my office."

He shrugged. “The door was open.”

“And that gives you the right to just walk in? I could have been with a client.”

“In that case, I would hope you’d be professional enough to shut the door for privacy. But you aren’t with a client *and* you knew I was coming back, so stop making a big deal out of it,” he said, stepping into her office and closing the door behind him.

Summer just stared at him for a moment, wondering how on earth the two of them were supposed to get along. Of course, whoever hired him had no idea they knew each other, and there was no way she could go to anyone at the TCC and request that they swap security companies without a valid reason.

“Look, Darius. You have a job to do and so do I. Evidently, I’m the last person you expected to see today. However, we’re professionals and are mature enough to make the best of it. It shouldn’t take you more than a day at the most to finish up here and—”

“Wrong.”

She lifted her brow. “Excuse me?”

He crossed his arms over his chest. “I said you’re wrong. Finishing up things here will take me every bit of a week. Possibly two.”

His words hit her like a ton of bricks. “You’ve got to be kidding.”

“I don’t kid.”

She pressed her lips together to keep from saying, *No, but you do kiss and tell.* Instead, she asked, “Why will it take *that* long to install a security system?”

There was a pause. A long pause. And for a moment, she wasn't sure he was going to answer her.

"The reason it will take so long is because in addition to installing a new security system on all the computers in this building, I'll be setting up a billing system for the Texas Cattleman's Club. I'm getting paid well to do a good job and I don't intend to do otherwise by rushing through things just to make your life less miserable."

"My life isn't miserable," she all but snapped.

"Sorry. It was foolish of me to assume that it was. And I see you're not wearing a ring so I guess you didn't get a rich husband after all."

Summer wondered what he was talking about and decided she really didn't want to know. "Look, Darius—"

He moved to her desk so quickly she jerked back in her chair. He placed his palms down on her desk and leaned over, his face within inches of hers. "No, you look, Summer. You're right, we are two professionals. Two adults who just happened to have had an affair that led to nowhere. I'm over it and so are you. So let's move on."

"Fine," she snapped.

"Great." He straightened his tall form, moved away from her desk and looked at a closet door across the room. "Unfortunately, the mainframe is in this office so I'll be spending more time in here than any other place. You might be inconvenienced a few times."

"If I'm scheduled to meet with clients, I'll use one

of the vacant conference rooms," she said, trying to keep her voice civil.

He nodded. "And if you're not scheduled to meet with a client?"

"I have the ability to work through distractions."

He lifted a brow and held her gaze for a moment. "Do you?"

"Yes."

"Then we don't have anything to worry about," he said, looking at his watch. "Are you meeting with a client sometime today?"

"No, I just have paperwork to do. Will you be shutting down my computer?" She could tell they were both trying to be courteous and hold a decent conversation in less-than-biting tones. But in spite of everything, she couldn't stop the sensations that stirred inside of her every time she looked into his eyes.

"No, but if that changes I'll give you advanced warning."

"Thank you."

He moved to the other side of the room. "Right now I need to get into this closet."

She swallowed as she stared at him under her lashes. His hands were on his hips, unconsciously drawing emphasis to his jean-clad hips and thighs. Tapered. Perfectly honed.

Deciding she had seen enough—probably too much—she picked up a file off her desk, leaned back in her chair and began reading. She tried like heck to concentrate on the document in front of her, but every so often she would look up and glance over at Darius. He was standing in front of a huge unit that had a bunch of wires running from it. He was concentrating on the computer's mainframe but her eyes were concentrated on him, drinking him in with feminine appreciation. He might be an arrogant ass but he was a good-looking one.

And as if he could feel her eyes on him, he looked up and met her gaze. Their eyes held for a moment longer than necessary before she dropped hers back to the document in front of her, thinking, *so much for working through distractions.*

Darius stared at Summer. Although he wished he were anyplace else other than here, he couldn't stop looking at her and remembering. She had gone back to reading, so he let his gaze travel over her, noticing the way her shoulder-length hair had fallen in her face. She absently brushed it back, giving him a view of her face once again. It was a face that had been his downfall the first time he'd seen it.

He could vividly recall just when that had been. After crawling through her bathroom window, she had seen him before Whitman had known he was in the house. With eye contact, Darius had encouraged her to stay calm and not give him away. Using the training he'd acquired, it had taken only a couple of quick kicks to bring Whitman down. He hit the ground before he'd realized what had happened to him.

It was then that a nearly traumatized Summer had

rushed into his arms, holding on to him as if her life depended on it. Even after the police officers had rushed in and handcuffed Whitman, she had still held on to him, like she was too shaken to let him out of her sight. Since it had been almost quitting time, he had followed the squad car that had taken her to the hospital to get checked out. He'd also dropped by her place the next day to repair her broken window.

During the weeks that followed, he would find some excuse or other to see her, and when he'd learned that her ex had been let out on bail, he had made it a point to drive by her house a couple of times a night just to make sure she was okay. Most of the time they would sit in her living room and talk.

During that time Summer had shared a lot about her life. He knew she had been raised by an aunt and that she had left her hometown of Birmingham, Alabama, for California with dreams of becoming an actress or, better yet, to find a rich older man to marry. At the time he'd thought she was teasing, but he'd discovered a few months later she'd been dead serious.

He'd found out the hard way that while he had been falling in love with her, she had been looking for a man with a lot more money than he'd had.

He fought back the anger that tried consuming him all over again, anger that seven years hadn't erased. He must have muttered something under his breath because she looked up and again their eyes met.

He tried looking away but couldn't. And when he moved to close the closet he told himself to head straight for the door and walk out. However, he couldn't do that, either.

Instead, he found himself crossing the room to where she was sitting. Although he had tried to forget it, he was still bothered by the fact that she had left him for another man. A man who had been old enough to be her father from what he'd heard.

By the time he reached her, she was standing. "What is wrong with you?" she asked, backing away from him until her back hit a solid wall and she couldn't go any farther.

His lips curved into a forced smile. "There's nothing wrong with me, Summer."

"Then what do you think you're doing?" she asked in a whisper.

"You still ask too many questions," he murmured, just seconds before leaning in and capturing her mouth with his.

The instant their mouths touched it registered in Summer's brain that she didn't have to accept his kiss. She could outright refuse it. However, any thoughts of doing so tumbled from her mind as he expertly took control of her mouth in a way she remembered so well.

His tongue surged between her parted lips and the moment it tangled with hers, she was a goner. Instead of being swamped with memories of the past, she was overtaken by sensations from the present, where he was causing a stir within her so effortlessly.

And it wasn't just about tongue play; it was a lot more than that. It was about body heat and the way she felt pressed against him, with his arms wrapped firmly around her waist and hers finding their way around his neck.

And then it was about a need. She could not characterize his, but she could certainly define her own. It had been seven years since she had been kissed by a man. Seven years of denying herself this one particular pleasure as well as numerous others. Those denials, especially the primal ones, were coming back to haunt her in the worst kind of way, thanks to him.

And then, she thought, when he pulled her body closer to his, closer to his heat, there was the idea, the very fact, that after all this time she was still attracted to him and he to her. Some things couldn't change. There was the chemistry, physical attraction, sexual tension. Lust was a strong benefactor, especially when motivated and fueled by sexual need.

He changed the angle of his mouth to deepen the kiss and tightened his hold around her waist. And then he used his tongue to taste her in a way he'd never done before. It was as if he were trying to get reacquainted with her flavor, sliding his tongue from one side of her mouth to the other.

Then, in a move she could only deem as sensuously strategic, he captured her tongue with his and began mating with it in a way that nearly brought her to her knees. He was building desire within her, slowly escalating their fiery exchange. Her hands moved from his neck to his shoulders, and then she spread her palms over his back as he elicited a response from her that she felt in every pore of her body.

Despite the greedy protest of her lips, he finally pulled his mouth away from hers. She drew in a much-needed breath. The kiss had been totally unexpected—completely without warning—and had managed to leave her breathless, speechless, with her senses heightened to their full capacity.

And then reality returned. She stiffened, determined that he would not assume the kiss would be the first of many, or that he was on the verge of finding his way back into her heart with the sole purpose of finding his way back into her bed.

Too late she began berating herself for letting the kiss last as long as it had. He was staring at her and she wondered if the kiss—especially the intensity of it—had been some kind of point he'd wanted to make. Probably, but she had news for him.

"If you want to keep your job, Darius, I would advise you to never do that again," she said in a cutting tone. "If you do, I will report your actions to the Texas Cattleman's Club. I'm sure there are other security companies they could use to do what you were hired to do."

She thought she saw a smile touch his lips before his gaze narrowed slightly. "Does it matter that you kissed me back? Moaned in my ear? Rubbed your body against mine?" he asked with a hint of scorn in his voice.

Summer felt heat flush her cheeks. Had she actually done all those things while they'd been kissing? Okay, she had returned his kiss, possibly even moaned a few times in his ear, but had she really rubbed her body against his? Due to the intensity of the exchange, that may very well have been a possibility. But that didn't mean she'd given him free rein to enjoy her mouth anytime the mood suited him. She needed to make sure he understood that.

"Fair warning, Darius. Kevin Novak of the TCC will be meeting with me this week to see how things are going at the shelter, and we'll be discussing ways that things around here can be improved. I'm sure getting this job was a feather in your cap and I'd hate to ask that you be replaced, but I will if you don't keep your hands to yourself."

His gaze locked on to hers for longer than necessary, and then he stepped back. Evidently, he realized she hadn't just made an idle threat. There was a long silence as they stood there staring at each other and then to her surprise, he smiled and said, "You enjoyed that kiss just as much as I did and I will bring up that fact to Mr. Novak if he questions me about anything. If you're thinking about putting me on the hot seat, then be ready to join me there. The TCC hired you to do a job, just like they hired me."

His dark eyes hardened. "And need I remind you that I've been living in Somerset a lot longer than you have? People around here know I'm a professional who's selective when it comes to friends. I have a tarnish-free reputation. This is a nice town, close-knit. You're the stranger here, Summer, not me. But I will heed your wishes. The next kiss, you'll initiate. Until then, you're safe with me."

She lifted her chin, wondering when he had become so arrogant, so sure of himself. For him to assume she would make a move on him was outright preposterous. "That won't happen."

He smiled. "Then I guess that means you're safe with me."

She was about to give him a blistering retort when his cell phone rang. "Excuse me," he said, and Summer watched as he quickly pulled it from his belt clip. She figured it was probably some woman calling him.

He muttered a few words to the caller and then glanced back at her and said, "I need to take this call. Remember what I said." And then he turned and walked out of her office.

Darius strolled into the lobby of the shelter, a safe distance from Summer's office, yet close enough so he could see if she left. He pulled in a deep breath and then remembered he had Kevin holding on the phone.

"Okay, Kev, I can talk now. What's up?"

"Just a reminder we're meeting at the TCC's game room Thursday night to shoot pool."

Darius couldn't help but grin. If Kev was calling to remind everyone, that meant he was feeling lucky. "I won't forget."

"Where are you?" Kevin asked.

"At Helping Hands. I decided to install the security system myself since I'm the one who's going to set up TCC's billing account for the shelter. Besides, all my men are handling other projects."

Darius then remembered something. "Your name came up in a conversation I had with the social worker here, Summer Martindale. You're supposed to meet with her sometime this week."

"Yeah, don't remind me. That was something Huntington was supposed to do and he delegated it to me like he's the king and I'm one of his lowly subjects. That man really grates on my last nerve."

Darius understood just how Kevin felt. He, Lance, Mitch and Justin all felt the same way. The five of them, along with Alex Montoya, were the most recent inductees into the Texas Cattleman's Club. This didn't sit well with some of the club's old guards—namely Sebastian Huntington and his stuffy cohorts—who for some reason felt the younger men really weren't deserving of membership in what was known as the most exclusive social club in the state of Texas.

"Hey, man, I thought all of us agreed to just overlook Huntington and his band of fools," Darius reminded his friend.

"Yeah, but he just rubs me the wrong way at times. He doesn't want to put his full support behind the shelter since the funding of it was our idea and not his."

"But he was outvoted, so eventually he'll get over it," Darius said. "And if he doesn't, then that's too bad. Maybe it's a good thing that he's having you do it instead of him. He wouldn't do anything but find fault with everything anyway."

"You're probably right. So, you've met Ms. Martindale?"

"Yes. She's the Summer I was involved with before moving here to Somerset."

"Damn, man, she's *that* Summer?"

"Yes, she is *that* Summer." Kevin didn't know as much about what had happened as Lance, but both of his best friends knew Summer had screwed him over in a bad way, which was the reason he'd wanted to leave Houston and start a new life here in Somerset.

"I need you to do me a favor," he said to Kevin.

"Sure. What do you need?"

It had always been this way between him, Lance and Kevin since their college days. Kevin had agreed to the favor without even knowing what would be required of him. The three trusted each other implicitly. "I'll go into full details when I see you Thursday night, but when you meet with Summer Martindale, if my name comes up, I don't want it mentioned that I'm affiliated with the TCC."

"No problem."

Darius had made the decision to tell Summer the truth when he was good and ready. He couldn't wait to see her face when she realized he was probably just as wealthy as the old man she had left him for.

He and Kevin began talking about the update he'd gotten on the fire at the Brody refinery. Darius was listening to Kevin's take on why he thought Alex Montoya was responsible when he heard footsteps on the tile floor. He glanced up to see Summer walking out of her office. He was standing behind a pillar, so she didn't have a full view of him, which to his way of thinking was a good thing. That way he could check her out at his leisure.

She walked over to a row of file cabinets and he quickly recalled that he'd always thought her walk was a turn-on. There was a sexy sway to her hips with every step she took. She was wearing a pair of brown slacks and a light blue blouse. The lush curves of her hips and the firm swell of her breasts were outlined to perfection by her outfit. He couldn't help standing there staring, taking in everything about her. He easily picked up on the differences in her, differences that, considering everything, he still couldn't help but appreciate.

She seemed a lot more self-assured, had taken ownership of her life and didn't easily back down from a fight. She certainly didn't have any problems trying to put him in his place earlier. The key word was *trying*. As far as he was concerned, when it came to her, he didn't have a place, especially not one she could put him in.

He should not have kissed her. But in all honesty, he could not have *not* kissed her. And now that he had, he wanted to kiss her again. Hold her in his arms. Take her to bed.

Darius tightened his hand in a fist at his side, not liking the way his thoughts were going and liking even less that he wanted to do those things with the same woman who had crushed his heart. But her response to the kiss had caught him off guard—her complete surrender had made him hard in a way he hadn't been in years.

He had forced himself to end the kiss before he'd taken a mind to do something stupid like take her on her desk. He had been that far gone and she had been right there with him, although she'd gotten a little hot behind the collar later.

"Darius? You still there?"

His concentration was pulled back into the phone conversation, and he was trying like heck to recall what Kevin had just said. "Look, Kev, I'll get back with you later. There's something I need to do before it gets too late."

"Sure, man."

After snapping the phone shut, Darius walked toward Summer. She glanced in his direction with a surprised look on her face. "I thought you had left."

He forced a smile. "I'm sure you were hoping so, but I'm not the type who takes off without letting a person know why, unless there is reason outside of my control. Not like some people."

She glared at him. "And just what is that supposed to mean?"

"Think about it. When you do, it won't take you long to figure things out. I'll be back tomorrow."

Without giving her a chance to say anything else, he walked away.

* * *

Darius tried to keep his composure as he eased his long legs into his car. Moments later, after he'd driven away from the shelter and was headed toward home, he let out the expletive that he'd been holding back. Summer was certainly playing the innocent act well, having the gall to pretend she hadn't a clue what he was talking about when he'd thrown out his dig. He couldn't help but wonder what else she was concealing. For all he knew she could very well know about his vast wealth or his membership in the TCC.

He tightened his grip on the steering wheel. Despite the deep animosity he was feeling toward her, his body refused to deny that it wanted her. She could stir embers of passion within him without saying a word. All it took was a look, her presence or her scent to bring his libido to full awareness. He had to do something about her. She had invaded his comfort zone. His space.

For six years he'd been living in Somerset, enjoying peace and harmony. Of all the cities for her to relocate to, why Somerset? Avoiding her wasn't an option, although it would make his life a whole heck of a lot easier. Her very presence unsettled him in the worst way.

He breathed in deeply and fought back the anger that was getting him riled all over again. If she wanted to pretend, then two could play that game. He was in a position to teach her the very lesson she deserved to learn. She'd wanted a rich husband and in his own way, he would let her know just how she'd lost out on one. He would bide his time, get on her good side and then, when she assumed things were going great between them, after he'd gotten her back in his bed, he would do the very same thing to her that she had done to him.

Walk away without looking back.

# Three

The following morning, with butterflies floating around in her stomach, Summer swiped her security card through the scanner before stepping into the shelter, hoping she was early enough to have arrived before Darius. He was the last person she wanted to see. She hadn't gotten much sleep last night and he was the reason. She'd been unable to get the kiss they'd shared yesterday out of her head.

As she made her way toward her office, she refused to even consider the reason why she'd taken more time getting dressed this morning than she usually did. Why she had spent a good ten minutes more putting on her makeup and why had she pulled out the curling iron for the first time in weeks.

When she stopped at Marcy's desk, she checked her watch. Marcy wasn't due in for another hour or so. Summer unlocked Marcy's desk to retrieve a clipboard that listed all her appointments and meetings for that day. Perusing the clipboard, she began to see what her day was going to be like.

"You look nice today."

Summer didn't bother to turn around. She didn't have to. She had left home with a made-up mind that no matter what, she was not going to let Darius rattle her. She was not going to allow him to make her come unglued and she would not look for condescension in his every word. So with that resolve, she would take his compliment in stride and assume he meant no more by it than what was said.

She turned around and her hands automatically tightened on the clipboard the moment she did so. She then swallowed deeply as the nervous sensations stirring in her stomach escalated. How was it possible that he looked even better today than yesterday? He was casually but impeccably dressed. A different pair of jeans and a different shirt, but the utterly breathtaking look was still there. All lean. Well-defined muscles. Perfect abs. And with the tan-colored Stetson sitting on his head, tilted at an angle that shadowed his dark brows, she couldn't help but admit he was truly a fine, handsome specimen of a man.

"Thank you for the compliment. You look nice, also," she heard herself say, determined not to get in a sparring match with him. "Will you need to be in my office today?"

"No, I'll be working in the other offices the majority of the day, other than when I start setting up the accounting for the TCC. It will be a while before I start on that."

She nodded, not wanting to prolong her time with him. "Then I guess I need to let you get started."

"How about lunch?"

She stared up at him, certain she had misunderstood. "Excuse me?"

He smiled and she felt a semblance of heat stirring in her blood, through her veins, in a number of other places she didn't want to think about. "I asked if you wanted to do lunch with me."

"Why?" She couldn't help but ask.

"Why not? You gotta eat and so do I."

"But that doesn't mean we have to share a meal," she pointed out.

His smile widened and the heat stirring in her blood intensified. "No, but it would mean that we're trying to put the past behind us and move on," he said. "It's not like we're going to become bosom buddies, because we aren't. But I'll be hanging around here for the next couple of weeks, so we might as well learn how to get along. I'm not going anywhere and I doubt you are, either. So, what about lunch?"

"I'm not sure that would be a good idea, Darius."

"What was it that you said yesterday? Oh, yes, your very words were, 'We're professionals and are mature enough to make the best of it.'"

Summer breathed in deeply. Yes, those had been her very words.

"I promise not to bite."

She opened her mouth to say something and changed her mind, quickly shutting it. A twist of emotions rumbled in her chest and she knew why. Darius was offering the olive branch, the chance to move on and put what they'd once shared behind them since there was no way it could ever happen again. And deep down she knew she needed that.

She couldn't continue carrying the bitterness of the last seven years. If they were doomed to live in the same town and would be running into each other on occasion, at least they could be civil to each other. But there was no chance of them ever getting back together. For her, the pain had gone too deep.

"Lunch will be fine," she heard herself say, hoping she didn't live to regret it.

"Great. You pick the place, just as long as they sell good hamburgers."

She couldn't help the smile that touched her lips. Some things evidently never changed and his love for hamburgers was one of them. "Too much ground beef isn't good for you," she said, quoting what she'd told him over a hundred times in the past.

And as expected, he rolled his eyes. "Yeah, yeah, I know, and the key words are *too much.* I've become a physical fitness addict, so I don't indulge in too many things that aren't good for me, but there's nothing wrong with enjoying a big, juicy hamburger every once in a while."

Summer decided not to say anything more on the matter. It was evident by his perfect body that he was into physical fitness. "I guess not. I'll be in the lobby at noon."

Darius stretched his neck to work out the kinks as he leaned back in the chair, away from the computer. He glanced up at the clock. It was almost noon.

He stood and stretched his entire body, refusing to acknowledge the anticipation he felt over joining Summer for lunch. Instead, he tried convincing himself that his nerves were the result of knowing he was slowly but surely breaking down her defenses and in good time, he would have the upper hand.

He was leaving the small office when his ears picked up the sound of commotion coming from the front of the building, near the lobby. He quickened his stride and when he rounded the corner, he saw a man standing outside the building with a baseball bat in his hand, threatening to break the glass door if he wasn't allowed to come in to get his wife and children. Summer, Darius saw, was talking to the man on the intercom, trying to reason with him.

He watched her, amazed at how calmly she was speaking to the man, clearly determined not to get ruffled by the vulgar language he was using and the threats he was making.

He glanced over at Marcy, who was sitting at her

desk. "Have the police been called?" he asked, shifting his attention back to the scene being played out a few feet away. "And where the hell is security?" he continued, keeping his gaze fixed on Summer. She continued to appear composed as she tried to settle the man down and convince him to go away.

"The police are on their way. Our security guard called in sick this morning."

Darius looked at Marcy. "They didn't send a replacement?"

"Not yet."

Darius frowned. Huntington and his group had voted against the idea of Darius's firm being in charge of all the security for the shelter. Instead, Huntington had recommended a security company the TCC had used in the past, claiming it was top-notch. The majority of the members had gone along with him except for Lance, Kevin, Mitch and Justin. When they had been outvoted, as a compromise, they had pushed for the club to consider Darius to handle the security for all the computers and to set up the billing system.

Huntington had fought hard against it, saying Darius was too new to the club to take on such tasks, but he had lost the fight when Alex Montoya had sided with them instead of Huntington's group. Darius got the feeling that in addition to the bad blood between Alex and the Brodys, there was bad blood between Alex and Huntington. But then it seemed Huntington had a beef against anyone under the age of forty who joined the club.

The sound of breaking glass recaptured Darius's attention and in a flash he raced forward and placed himself in front of Summer just as the man who was wielding the bat forced his way through the broken glass toward her.

"Be a man and hit me instead of a woman. I dare you," Darius snarled through gritted teeth, not trying to hide the searing rage coursing through him.

The man evidently thought twice about following through on Darius's offer and dropped the bat, taking a step back. Within seconds, the shelter was swarming with police officers. Two of them quickly came through the broken glass door to apprehend the man, who didn't put up a fight.

Darius turned to Summer. "Are you all right?" he asked in a low voice. He hadn't realized just how angry he was until now. If that man had harmed a single strand of hair on her head, Darius would have gone ballistic.

In a way, Darius wished the man had taken him up on his offer. That would have given him the excuse he needed to flatten him. The man had just proven what a coward he was. He was willing to take a bat to a woman, but had wasted no time backing away instead of squaring off with a man equal to his size and weight.

He watched Summer breathe in deeply. "Yes, I'm fine. It's not unusual for a husband to show up wanting to see his wife and children, and when we tell them they can't, most move on. Once in a while, we get someone like Mr. Green who refuses to abide by our rules and causes problems. Usually when that happens, security handles it."

Darius nodded. He would be calling a special meeting of the TCC to make sure something like this didn't happen again. He didn't want to think what could have happened had he not been there. There was no doubt in his mind that the man intended to use that bat on someone.

Before he could say anything, a police officer approached them to obtain their statements. After recording all the facts, the officer advised Summer that she would need to go down to police headquarters so formal charges against the man could be filed.

No sooner had the officer walked away than a woman Darius recognized as a staff member walked up. "Excuse me, Ms. Martindale, but some of the women are upset. They heard a man was trying to force his way inside."

Summer nodded. "Okay, I'm on my way to meet with them."

She then turned back to Darius. "Thanks for your help. I really didn't think he would go so far as to break down the glass. I was hoping that I'd be able to talk some sense into him."

She glanced at her watch. "I need to calm down the women and then go to the police station. I guess lunch is off now."

He shook his head. "No, it's not. Go meet with the women and then I'll drive you to headquarters. Afterward, on the way back, we'll grab something to eat."

"Okay. Thanks." She started to walk away and then glanced at all the glass around the door.

"Go on. I'll make sure this mess is cleaned up and get the glass replaced," he said.

She gave him an appreciative smile before hurrying off with the staff member.

When she'd rounded the corner, Darius released a curse and pulled the cell phone from his belt, hitting the speed dial for Lance's number. His best friend answered on the first ring. "Hey, what's up, Darius?"

"There was an incident here at the shelter and security was not in place. We need to call a TCC meeting."

"I thought we were never going to get out of there," Summer said as they left police headquarters. Darius led her over to his car.

After calming down the women and children, she'd had to meet personally with Gail Green to let her know what her husband had done. Then Summer had to assure Gail that the shelter wouldn't be putting her and her two children out because of the incident.

Gail and her two little boys had arrived at the shelter three days ago after fleeing from their home in the middle of the night. The bruises on her body were evidence enough that she'd been in an abusive situation, but like a number of other women who sought refuge at the shelter, she had refused to press charges.

"I thought they handled everything in a timely manner," Darius said, smiling faintly as he opened the car door for her.

She rolled her eyes. "Spoken like a true ex-cop."

He chuckled before closing her door and moving around the car to the other side. The clock on his console indicated it was after three and they still hadn't eaten lunch.

"Where to?" he asked when he got settled behind the wheel with his seat belt in place. "And don't say back to the shelter because it won't happen. I'm taking you somewhere so we can grab something to eat. I'm hungry even if you're not."

As if on cue, her stomach growled and Summer couldn't help but grin. "Sorry. I guess that means I'm hungry, too. Have you tried that café around the corner from the shelter? The Red Sky."

"No. I've passed by it a few times but have never eaten there."

"Then I guess this is your lucky day because that's where I want to go."

"All I want to know is do they make good hamburgers?" he asked, easing his car into traffic.

"I've never eaten one of their burgers. I'm a salad girl."

He glanced over at her and grinned. "So, you haven't kicked that habit?"

"You want to consult Dr. Oz to determine which of us is eating healthier?"

"No."

She couldn't help but laugh. "I figured as much."

It felt good to laugh. She would never admit it to anyone, especially to Darius, but Samuel Green had truly frightened her and she was glad Darius had been there. When Mr. Green had burst through that door after breaking the glass, she'd had flashbacks to that time with Tyrone when she'd been exposed to his true colors. She had seen his anger out of control, and that anger had been directed at her. A backhand blow had sent her sprawling across the room but she had been quick enough to make it to the door before he could do anything else.

That had been the one and only time Tyrone had raised a hand to her, and she made sure it was the last. A courier had returned her engagement ring to him in the same box it had come in and later that same day, he'd been notified of the restraining order she'd filed. Thinking about it now, she appreciated the fact that she'd gotten out of an abusive situation. She had known when it was time to part ways even if Tyrone hadn't.

She glanced over at Darius. "Did you get much work done today?"

He shrugged. "Not as much as I would have liked, but that's okay. Typically, a job of this sort wouldn't take a whole lot of time, but security is a concern at the shelter, as it should be."

There was no way she would argue with that.

"And as far as the billing system goes," he continued, "I understand the TCC has money, but they want a firm accounting of how their money is being spent."

"Yes, and rightly so," she said, wondering if he thought she felt otherwise. "This shelter is fortunate to be funded by such a distinguished group of men. Do you know any of them?"

He lifted a brow. "Any of whom?"

"Members of the TCC?"

"Why would I know any of them?"

She noted that he sounded offended by her question. "I didn't mean if you knew them personally. I was just wondering if you've ever met any of them. After all, you were hired by them."

He didn't say anything for a moment. "Yes, I've met some of them. They're okay for a bunch of rich guys, and I respect the club for all the things they do in the community. It's my understanding that some of the members prefer not having their identities known. They like doing things behind the scenes without any recognition."

Summer nodded. She could respect that, knowing there were a number of wealthy people who preferred being anonymous donors. She appreciated everything the TCC had done so far and all the things they planned to do. She was definitely looking forward to her meeting with Mr. Novak on Friday. Presently, Helping Hands could accommodate up to fifteen women and children that needed shelter care. Already the TCC had plans in the works to expand the shelter's facilities to triple that amount.

"You've gotten quiet," he said.

She glanced over at Darius and couldn't help but feel a rush of gratitude. He had stood back and let her handle things until the situation had gotten out of control. She appreciated his intervening when he did, playing the role of knight in shining armor once again.

She continued looking at him. His eyes were on the road and her mind couldn't help but shift to another time when he'd been driving her someplace. It had been their first official date. They had gone out for pizza and afterward he had taken her home. She had invited him inside and later, sitting beside him on the sofa, the kissing had begun. A short while later she had been lying beneath him in her bed as he made love to her in a way she hadn't known was possible. The intensity of the memories of that night was almost enough to push everything that had happened over the past seven years into the background.

Almost, but not quite.

"Summer?"

She blinked when she realized they had come to a traffic light and he had glanced over at her, catching her staring. "Yes?"

"Are you sure you're okay? I guess incidents such as what happened earlier are expected to some degree, which is the reason I'm installing state-of-the-art security software on all the computers—to reduce the risk that the location of the women seeking refuge is discovered. But still, it has to be unnerving when one of the husbands or boyfriends shows up."

*If you only knew.* "Yes, and what's really sad is the fact that the women have to go into hiding at all. The Greens have two beautiful little boys and today their father showed up demanding them back with, of all things, one of their baseball bats. The person we saw today was not a loving father or husband but a violent and dangerous man."

Summer frowned and then she sighed deeply. Tonight she would get a good night's sleep and try to forget the incident ever happened. Fat chance. She would remember it and she would imagine what could have happened had Darius not been there.

"Here we are."

She looked around. Darius had pulled into the café's parking lot and brought the car to a stop. She glanced over at him. He was staring at her with an intensity that sent shivers of awareness through her body.

Sexual chemistry was brewing between them again. She could feel his body heat emanating from across the car. Summer forced the thought to the back of her mind.

"Umm, I guess we should go on inside," she forced her mouth to say. The way he was looking at her made her want to suggest that they go somewhere else, but she fought the temptation and held tight to her common sense.

She decided now was as good a time as any to thank him. "I really do appreciate what you did today, Darius, and I want to—"

"No, don't thank me."

His words stopped her short. "Why?"

"Because I didn't do any more than what was needed. No more than any other man would have done."

She contemplated his words. He was a man of action. Twice she had seen him in full swing and neither time had he accepted her words of gratitude. "I *will* thank you, Darius Franklin, because you deserve to be thanked."

And before he could respond, she got out of the car.

"Hey, Ms. Martindale, do you want your usual spot?" Tina asked when Summer walked in.

"Whatever is available," Summer answered, feeling the heat of Darius's chest close to her back. His nearness was almost unsettling.

"You must come here often," he said, moving to stand at her side.

She glanced over at him and smiled. "Practically every day. It's not far from the shelter and I enjoy the walk. And I like their grilled chicken salads."

Moments later they were being escorted to a table in the rear. Darius shifted his full attention to the people whose tables they passed. They either greeted her by name or smiled a hello. "You're pretty popular, I see," he said when they had taken their seats.

She shrugged. "Most are regulars who know that I work at the shelter. They believe it benefits the community and appreciate our presence."

They halted conversation for a while to scan the menu. Darius was the one deciding what he wanted since Summer was getting her usual. However, she was inclined to check out the soup of the day, or at least pretend that she was doing so. It was hard concentrating on anything, even food, while sitting across from Darius. As he studied his menu, she studied him over the top of hers.

She almost laughed out loud at the intense expression on his face. Deciding what hamburger he wanted couldn't be all that serious. But then Darius had always been a very serious man. Especially when it came to making love.

For a heart-flipping moment she wondered why a memory like that had crossed her mind, but she knew. Darius was the kind of man that oozed sexuality as potent as it could get, making those incredible urges consume the lower part of her body. They'd only had one night together, but it had been incredible. No matter what had happened after that, she could not discount how he'd made her feel.

He was the most gifted of lovers. Pleasing her had seemed to be the most natural thing in the world to Darius. She hadn't realized just how selfish Tyrone had been in the bedroom until after she'd made love to Darius. How could she have realized when Tyrone had been her first? No matter what her sexual experience had been with Tyrone, one time with Darius had made everything just fine.

Darius glanced up and she took in a lungful of air. The intensity of his gaze—she wanted to look away, but she couldn't. It was as if she were held captive by his deep, dark eyes.

"Here are your waters."

Summer almost jumped when Tina appeared with

two glasses of water. "Thanks." Barely giving her a chance to set the glass down in front of her, Summer picked it up and took a long gulp, feeling the need for the ice-cold water to cool her down.

Tina hung around long enough to take their food and drink order before moving on again.

"So, what do you like about your job?"

She glanced over at him to answer his question, making an attempt to keep her gaze trained on his nose instead of his eyes. "Everything, but mostly the satisfaction I get from helping women in distress, those who might feel broken up because of what has happened. I like letting them know they aren't alone and somebody cares."

What she didn't add was that she enjoyed giving them the same support he had given her during those first crucial days, when she had begun doubting herself, second-guessing the situation and believing that maybe she had been the cause of Tyrone's problems instead of the other way around.

"I notice there's not a director at the shelter," he said.

Her gaze drifted down from his nose to his lips. Focusing on his mouth was just as bad as looking into his eyes. He had a sexy mouth. It was a mouth that could move with agonizing slowness when talking… or when being used for other things. She swallowed before responding.

"When I was hired by the TCC it was decided that I could handle it all for now. When they complete the proposed expansions and decide to fill the position, I'm hoping I'll be considered for the job."

Darius nodded. He had not been a part of the TCC committee that had done the hiring for Helping Hands, which was one of the reasons he'd been surprised to discover her working there. He would have recognized her name the second it came across his desk.

"The shelter is pretty full now. How do you manage it all?" he asked.

She shrugged. "It's not so bad. I think the most challenging times are when I'm called in the middle of the night to a police station or hospital to comfort a woman who's been beaten or raped."

Darius's jaw twitched at the thought of anyone treating a woman so cruelly. Mistreatment of a woman was one thing he could not tolerate.

"It's also difficult at times when manning the abuse hotline. Someone is there to take calls twenty-four hours a day—usually a volunteer trained to do so. Every once in a while, a call will come through that I need to handle. Those are the ones that can get pretty emotional, depending on the circumstances."

Darius could tell from her voice that she was dedicated to what she did every day. To stay on safe ground and not stray on to a topic neither of them wanted to deal with, he decided to keep her talking about her work at the shelter.

For the first time since seeing her again, he was lowering his guard a little.

When the waitress finally delivered their order, he

had to admit the food looked good. And after a bite into his hamburger, he had to own up that it tasted good, too. One of his uncles in Charleston once owned a sandwich shop that used to make the best burgers around. As a kid, he enjoyed the summers he spent there and the older he got, he found himself comparing every hamburger he ate to his uncle Donald's. None could compare, but he had to admit this one came pretty close.

"How does it taste?"

He glanced over at Summer and could only smile and nod, since he couldn't talk with a mouth full of hamburger.

A half hour later, on the drive back to the shelter, he reflected on a number of things he hadn't expected. Mainly, he hadn't figured on sitting across from her for almost an hour and enjoying her company without animosity or anger seeping in. However, what couldn't be helped was the sexual tension. Although they had tried to downplay it with a lot of conversation, it was there nonetheless.

There was a lot about her he could barely resist. Her scent topped the list. Whatever perfume she was wearing filled his nostrils with a luscious fragrance that seemed to get absorbed right into his skin. And then there were her eyes. He was fully aware that she'd tried to avoid looking at him, which had been hard to do since they were sitting directly across from each other. Each time he would catch her staring at him, he would feel a pull in his stomach.

Thankfully, his hands were gripping the steering wheel because at that moment, it wouldn't take much for him to reach over and touch her, stroke that part of her thigh exposed beneath her skirt. Seeing her flesh peeking at him was making his mind spin, so he tried focusing on the road and decided to get her talking again. Anything to keep his mind off taking her.

"So, where do you live?" he asked.

He kept his gaze glued to the road. She didn't need to see the heat in his eyes, a telltale sign that although he wished otherwise, she was getting to him.

"I bought a house a block from the post office," she said.

He noted she didn't provide him with the name of her street. There were a couple of new communities sprouting up near the post office, as well as a number of newly renovated older homes that had been for sale. "Nice area," he heard himself say.

"I like it. My neighborhood's pretty quiet. Most of the people on my street are a lot older and are in bed before eight at night."

He nodded. From the information she had just shared he could safely assume that she had purchased one of the renovated homes in the older, established communities. Doing so had been a smart move on her part; they were a good investment.

She then opened up and began telling him about it, saying she was having a lot of fun decorating the house. He didn't find that hard to believe. When she'd lived in Houston, her apartment had been small but nice and he'd been surprised to learn she had done most of the decorating herself.

All too soon he was pulling into the parking lot of the shelter. "Thanks for taking me to lunch," she said, reaching to unsnap her seat belt even before he could bring the car to a complete stop. "Although I have to admit, riding in the car instead of walking only means I have to get my daily physical activity some other way," she added.

He came close to saying that he knew another way she could get her physical activity, and it would be something she would enjoy—he would make sure of it. Instead, he decided it would be best to keep his mouth shut.

"But since it will probably be dark when I leave today, I'll take the day off from exercise," she tacked on, getting out of the car.

He glanced over at her. "Why are you staying late?"

"Because I have a lot of work and can't leave until I'm finished. I'm meeting with Mr. Novak on Friday and there are a number of reports I have to run. More than likely, the TCC will have heard about the incident today and will want a full report on what happened."

He tightened his mouth after almost telling her that he'd already given them one. While at police headquarters, he had gotten a call from Mitch, Justin and Kevin. Lance had told them what had happened. Minor details had been given on television—since it was a women's shelter, no television crews or reporters were allowed to show up in order to protect the women staying there.

He knew if Summer stayed beyond five o'clock, she'd be pulling a long day. But for some reason, he had a feeling that was probably the norm for her. "Isn't there someone who can help you with those reports?"

"Afraid not. Besides, I'd rather run them myself, especially since I plan on pleading my case to Mr. Novak for an expansion of the shelter sooner rather than later."

Darius didn't say anything, but considering what had happened earlier that day, he wasn't crazy about her walking out to her car alone. Although the parking lot was well lit, he still didn't like it. Two security guards had shown up after the incident. He decided that before he left for the day, he would talk to the guards and make sure one of them walked Summer to her car.

When they reached the door he decided that unlike her, he intended to leave at a decent time. He had a meeting with the fire chief later, and it was a meeting he didn't want to miss. And besides, the last thing he needed was to end up in the office late at night with Summer—alone.

# Four

Darius grabbed a beer out of the refrigerator and popped the top before tilting the can to his mouth, appreciating the cool brew that flowed down his throat. When the can was empty, he scowled before crushing the aluminum and tossing it into the recycling bin.

His frown deepened as he sat down at the kitchen table, thinking that today had certainly not gone like he'd planned. He was convinced that the incident at the shelter was the prime reason his protective instincts toward Summer had kicked in. He had been ready to do bodily harm to anyone who even thought of hurting her. And he could admit that the reason he had driven her to police headquarters and then later to lunch was because he hadn't wanted her out of his sight. He was becoming attached again, and that wasn't good.

He rubbed a hand down his face. Maybe he needed to rethink the notion of exacting some sort of revenge on her and instead, just put distance between them and let it go at that, treating her the way he would other groupies or gold diggers whenever they crossed his path.

But he wasn't able to do that. If anything, today proved that when it came to Summer, he didn't think straight or logically. Right now, the only thing he should be thinking about was hurting her the way she had hurt him. Therefore, regardless of any protective instincts he might have, he would continue with his plan to make her think something special was going on between them. Then, at the right time, he'd drop the bomb that she meant nothing to him, and she'd discover she had gotten played, just like he had.

When his cell phone went off, he stood and pulled it off his belt. "What's up, Lance?" After his meeting with Chief Ingle, he had stopped by the TCC Café and had dinner with Kevin and Justin. Lance and his wife had driven to Houston to attend some sort of function there.

"I got your message. So Ingle thinks the fire was started with some sort of petroleum-based product?" Lance asked.

"He's pretty sure of it. But it wasn't one that could easily be detected, which is the reason the investigation took so long. They're trying to narrow the components down. However, he believes it's the same kind found in lubricating oils used for ranch equipment," Darius responded.

"Something that Montoya could easily get his hands on, since he owns that cattle ranch," Lance was quick to point out.

Darius shook his head. "His men are the ones working his ranch the majority of the time, Lance. Montoya's heavily involved in his import/export business."

"For crying out loud, Darius, you just don't want to believe he's responsible for that fire, do you?" Lance asked with frustration in his voice.

"What I don't want is for you to be so convinced Montoya is behind the fire that you start overlooking any other possible suspects."

"There aren't any other possible suspects, Darius. Montoya is the only one who hates me and Mitch bad enough to do such a thing. At the end of your investigation, you'll see that all the evidence points in Montoya's direction."

A few hours later, the fire investigation was the last thing on Darius's mind when he finally eased into bed, determined to get a good night's sleep. Moments later, after a number of tosses and turns, he discovered doing so wouldn't be easy when thoughts of Summer filled his mind. When he thought of what could have possibly happened had he not been there today. Even now he was worried that she was still at the center working, and he was tempted to go check for himself to make sure she was all right. But then he quickly recalled he had spoken with security to make sure someone escorted her to her car whenever she did work late.

He breathed in deeply, getting angry with himself that his concern for her, this feeling stirring deep within him, was making him weak. He refused to let that happen. But each time he closed his eyes, he saw her, remembered a better time between them, a time when she had been his whole world.

He stared up at the ceiling, determined to remember that she was not his whole world any longer, would never be it again. It was something he couldn't lose sight of. He would keep up his guard with her, no matter what.

"Thank you for walking me to my car, Barney, but it really wasn't necessary."

"No problem, ma'am. Besides, it was Mr. Franklin's orders."

Summer raised a brow at the uniformed guard. "Was it?"

"Yes."

Summer pondered that. How could Darius give an order to a guard who didn't work for him? Evidently, Barney had no problem following an order from someone who wasn't his boss.

"Well, good night," she said, opening her car door and getting inside.

"Just a minute, Ms. Martindale. This was pinned to your windshield beneath the wipers," he said, handing the piece of paper to her.

Summer tossed the flyer onto the seat beside her. "Good night."

"Good night."

Summer drove off, noticing Barney was still standing there, watching her pull out of the parking lot. No doubt he was still following Darius's orders. After what happened today, she could understand his concern and appreciated him wanting to make sure she was all right. Just like she had appreciated him taking her to lunch.

There had been something strange about sitting across from a man who had once undressed her, rubbed his hands all over her naked body and made love to her in a way that thinking about it took her breath away. A man who'd shown her that foreplay was an art form that could be taken to many levels, and that a person's mouth was just as lethal as his hands when making love.

When her car came to a stop at a traffic light, she turned on the radio, hoping the sound of music would drown out her thoughts of Darius. That wasn't going to happen, she thought, when she recalled how long after she'd left Houston she would lie in bed and think of him.

Her stomach growled and she remembered she'd missed dinner. When she got home she would make a sandwich and a glass of iced tea. It was one of those hot August nights.

As she waited for the light to change, she glanced over at the flyer she'd thrown on the seat and picked it up. Her breath caught in her throat and chills ran up her spine when she read the words, "I take care of my own."

The light turned green but she didn't realize it until the driver behind her blasted his horn. She accelerated, wondering which husband or boyfriend had placed the note on her car. It wouldn't be the first time one of the abusers of the women at the shelter blamed the staff for keeping his family from him. Mr. Green had taken the same position earlier that day. She wouldn't be surprised if it had been Mr. Green who had placed the note there, since her car had been parked in one of the spaces reserved for shelter personnel.

Summer tossed the paper aside, thinking of Mr. Green and the baseball bat, and his terrified wife. She sighed. She had long ago stopped trying to figure out why some men could treat a woman they claimed to love so shabbily.

The next day, Darius studied the computer screen in front of him and tried not to think about the woman a few doors down. She had been holed up in her office all morning and it was almost noon. He would bet any amount of money she would not be stopping for lunch.

A part of him knew it was really none of his business whether she ate or not, but another part decided to make it his business. Just as well, since he hadn't been able to concentrate worth a damn anyway.

Before arriving at the shelter, he had dropped by the refinery to take a look around the area damaged by the fire, hoping he would find something that had been overlooked previously. He hated admitting it, but Lance was right. All the evidence accumulated so far was pointing at Montoya, especially since the man didn't have an alibi for that night and he'd been seen in the vicinity of the refinery. However, the evidence was too cut-and-dried to suit Darius—way too pat. As far as he was concerned, if Montoya wasn't guilty, then someone who knew about the feud between Montoya and the Brodys was certainly making it look that way.

Darius stood as he checked his watch, deciding it was time to feed his stomach and satisfy his desire to see Summer again. He had fought the impulse to drop by her office and say hello when he had arrived at the shelter. But he couldn't fight it anymore.

Her office door had been closed, which meant she was either counseling someone or buried knee-deep in work. She had mentioned getting ready for that meeting tomorrow with Kev. But still, she had to eat, and he kind of enjoyed that café where they had eaten yesterday. The hamburger had been delicious.

Walking down the corridor, he went to the secretary's desk. "Is Ms. Martindale in a meeting with someone?" he asked Marcy.

Marcy stopped thumbing through a bunch of folders on her desk long enough to look up and smile at him. "No, she's going over some papers. If you need to talk with her about something, just knock on her door."

He returned her smile. "I think I will. Thanks."

Strolling back the way he'd come, he came to a stop in front of her door, hesitating a moment before knocking, convincing himself he was only pretending to be a nice guy when in fact, she really didn't deserve his kindness.

"Come in."

He opened the door and walked into her office, closing it behind him. She didn't look up. "Ready for lunch?" he asked.

She lifted her gaze from the document she'd been reading to fix it on him. The moment their eyes met, a slight tremor touched him. And if that weren't bad enough, he could feel a deep stirring in his gut. He stood there, fully conscious of the effect she was having on him and not liking it, but unable to do anything but stand there and take it like a man who wanted a woman, a woman he should have gotten from under his skin long ago. She broke eye contact with him and looked back down at the document she'd been reading. "I can't today."

*You can't or you won't?* Instead of asking, he said, "Yes, you can. You'll think better on a full stomach."

When she looked back up at him without saying anything, as if giving his words some serious thought, he decided to add, "Besides, that hamburger I ate yesterday was pretty good and—"

"And you probably don't need another one today. Too much beef," she finished for him, pushing her papers aside. "Why don't you try a salad?"

He chuckled. "That's rabbit food."

She rolled her eyes. "That's healthy." And then she said. "Okay, I'll have lunch with you, but only if we walk to the café."

He felt the amusement leave his face. "Walk?"

"Yes. Walk."

He noticed she was watching him intently, probably expecting him to back down. He couldn't help the smile that touched the corners of his lips when he said, "Fine. We'll walk."

"You really didn't expect me to do it, did you?"

Summer glanced over at Darius. They had been walking for the past few minutes in silence, which gave her the chance to wonder how, for the third day in a row, she'd been in his presence. He was right. She hadn't expected him to agree to walk to the café with her. Not that she thought he wasn't in any kind of shape to do so, but mainly because he didn't have a pair of walking shoes tucked away in a desk like she had. He was wearing cowboy boots, and they complemented his jeans and chambray shirt. And he had grabbed his Stetson off the rack to put on his head, which, considering the heat of the sun, had been a good idea. He looked good in his Western attire, too good to be walking with her on the dusty sidewalk. Every so often when someone needed to squeeze by them, Darius's denim-clad thigh would brush up against hers, making her very aware of the strength of his masculinity.

"No, I really didn't," she said finally. "But you have to admit it's a beautiful day outside. A perfect day to walk."

She couldn't help remembering the last time they had taken a walk together, late one afternoon when he'd shown up at her place after getting off work. They had strolled to the neighborhood park and on the way back had stopped at a corner store for ice-cream cones. That had been a perfect day to walk, too.

She breathed in deeply in an attempt to erase the memory from her mind. For three days, she had allowed him to invade her personal space and she wasn't exactly happy with the fact that he'd done so. She had appreciated his help yesterday, but somehow she needed to get him to understand that being cordial to each other didn't mean they had to share lunch every day.

"How is Aunt Joanne?"

She nearly missed a step and felt his hand on her elbow, reaching out to steady her, keeping her from falling. She stopped walking and glanced up at him. He was standing a scarce few inches in front of her and met her gaze. Darius had met Aunt Joanne when she had come to Houston to give Summer much-needed support during Tyrone's trial. Her aunt had liked Darius, and Summer wanted to believe that Darius had liked her aunt, as well, that his feelings toward Aunt Jo had been genuine and not fake—like the ones he'd displayed toward her.

"Summer, what's wrong?"

She swallowed and fought back the tears that threatened every time she thought of losing her aunt. "Aunt Jo died two years ago."

She saw surprise and then sorrow in his eyes. "I'm sorry. What happened? Was she ill?" he asked. He moved his hands from her elbow to her hand, and she could feel him wrapping his fingers around hers.

She shook her head. "No, in fact she'd had a physical the day before and had called to tell me how well it went, and that the doctor had even joked about her being fifty-five and would probably live well past ninety-five because she was in such good shape."

Summer paused a moment and then continued. "On her way home from work one night, she stopped at an ATM. A guy came up, demanding her money. She emptied her account and gave him all she had, but he shot and killed her anyway."

"Oh, Summer, I'm sorry to hear that," he said, pulling her into his arms. And she went without hesitation, ignoring the fact they were standing in the middle of the sidewalk. She was being given the shoulder to cry on that she had needed so badly two years ago. Burying her aunt had been the hardest thing she'd ever had to do. Less than a year after graduating from college, she'd lost the only person who'd been there for her consistently.

"That's it, Summer, get it all out," Darius urged gently in her ear. "Let it go." She felt the strength of his arms wrap around her shoulders, drawing her close.

Summer wasn't sure just how long she stood there, on a public street, being comforted by the only man she had ever loved—and who had done her wrong. She wasn't sure if she could ever forgive him for breaking her heart.

Pulling herself together, she eased back out of his arms, breaking all physical contact with him. "Sorry about that," she said softly.

"Don't apologize. Are you okay?"

"Yes, I'm fine." She nudged her hands into the pockets of her slacks and glanced down at the pavement. "It's still hard for me sometimes."

"I imagine that it would be, and I really meant it when I said that I'm sorry, Summer."

The sincerity in his voice as well as the warmth of his tone touched her in a way that it should not have. She lifted her head to glance back up at him. "Thank you."

"You're welcome."

As they continued their walk toward the café, Summer's head was spinning with confusion over whether she could trust this man who had crushed her heart once before but seemed filled with pure compassion for her. Should she listen to her head, her heart…her body? She suddenly felt like she was nineteen again, and she didn't like it at all. Not at all.

# Five

"You haven't been listening to a thing I've said," Justin Dupree complained while eyeing Darius curiously. The two men were enjoying a meal at one of the exclusive restaurants in town with plans to drop by the TCC later and play pool with Lance, Mitch and Kevin.

Darius took another sip of his beer and gave his friend an apologetic smile. "Sorry, what did you say?"

A smile touched the corners of Justin's lips. "I said Monica Cooper has been giving you the eye all night."

Darius raised a brow. "Who?"

Justin rolled his eyes. "Monica. You know. Sultry lips Monica."

Darius couldn't help but grin as he leaned back in

his chair and took another sip of his beer. "No, I don't know her, but I'm sure you do."

There weren't too many single women with sultry lips that Justin didn't know. He had a reputation of being Somerset's number one jet-setting playboy. Heir to his family's multimillion-dollar shipping company, Justin could probably talk a nun out of her clothes. He could also close any business deal he wanted—he had a reputation of being a tough-as-nails, ruthless businessman. Darius was proud to consider him a friend.

Justin smiled. "Yes, I know her. Her dad owns a nice spread outside of Austin. She comes to Somerset every summer to visit her aunt. She seems taken with you."

Darius didn't even bother looking over his shoulder at the woman. Instead, he said, "That's nice." He knew Justin had to be wondering why he wasn't showing Monica, or any woman for that matter, any interest tonight. Even their waitress had given him a flirty smile. But the only woman he could think about at the moment was the one he'd had lunch with today. The one he couldn't get out of his mind.

The one he had held in his arms while she'd cried.

"Okay, Darius, what's going on in that brain of yours? Lance said you still don't want to believe that Montoya was behind that fire."

Darius studied the contents of his beer bottle before glancing over at Justin. The two of them were best friends to the Brodys. Justin was Mitch's best friend like he was Lance's.

In a way, Darius felt guilty. He hadn't been thinking about Montoya and the fire, and he really should be. He had been thinking about Summer. But now that Justin had brought it up…

"I'm just not as convinced as everyone seems to be. Like you, Montoya is a shrewd businessman. Always on top of his game. Smart as a whip. I can't see him being stupid enough to set fire to his enemy's refinery, not when all fingers would point his way. He has no motive."

Justin shook his head. "Sure he does. You just said it. He and Lance are enemies."

"But that's just it, Justin. They have been enemies for years. That's nothing new. According to Lance, that goes as far back as high school. Competing against each other every chance they got."

"Yes," Justin said, "and they are still competing against each other today, in practically everything. The only reason Montoya decided to join the TCC was to be a deliberate thorn in Lance's side. On top of that, Montoya is friends with Paulo Ruiz, and everyone knows that guy has underworld connections and is as shady as they come. For all we know, Ruiz may have been the one to arrange the fire for Montoya."

Darius nodded, but he still wasn't convinced. "Well, all we got now is circumstantial evidence that wouldn't hold up in court. Unless there is valid proof, then—"

"I'll get it," Justin said, interrupting Darius.

Darius raised a dark brow. "And just how do you plan to do that?"

Justin smiled. "You'll find out when I lay all the evidence you need at your feet."

Hours later on the drive away from the TCC, Darius couldn't help but reflect on what Justin had said over dinner. Granted, he didn't know Montoya as well as the others since he hadn't lived in Somerset all his life, but he couldn't help but admire someone who had worked hard to propel himself from rags to riches. He'd heard that Montoya had once been a groundskeeper at the club.

And Darius had a hard time believing that someone that driven to succeed would risk losing it all in a situation where he would automatically be labeled the guilty party. Darius was convinced that if Montoya had been involved in the fire, he would have done a better job of covering his tracks. The man didn't even have a valid alibi, for crying out loud. Definitely not the stance of a guilty arsonist.

Darius decided that before going to bed he would go back over the information he had collected so far, especially his interviews with a number of employees who had left the company within the past couple of years on bad terms. He then cursed under his breath when he realized he'd left the file with his notes back at the shelter.

Darius turned on the radio, deciding he needed to hear some music. He let out a deep breath as he recognized the song as one that had been playing earlier today at the café while he and Summer had shared lunch.

The image of Summer sitting across from him as she tried to put the pain of losing her aunt behind her flooded his mind. He'd liked her aunt and thought it was tragic how the woman had lost her life. He could just imagine what Summer had gone through during that time. But he really didn't want to think about that. Then why was he? Why did he have to constantly remind himself that he couldn't—and shouldn't—care?

He glanced at the clock on his car's console. It was close to ten. Tomorrow he would spend the day at the refinery, checking out a few things and questioning a number of the employees, including one who claimed he saw someone fitting Montoya's description in the refinery's parking lot the night of the fire.

The moment he stopped at a traffic light, his cell phone went off. He quickly slid it open. "Yes?"

"Darius, this is Walt. I got a message that you called."

Darius smiled. Hearing his old partner's voice reminded him of working as a detective in Houston. They'd had some good times together, despite Walt's miserable attitude. "Yes, Walt, how are things going?"

"Pretty much the same. I'm sure you heard that Smothers finally retired. We were all glad about that."

"Yes, I heard." John Smothers was a tough detective who should have retired ages ago.

"So, what's up? You said you needed my help with something," Walt said.

"I'm investigating a case of arson here in Somerset

and need you to do a background check on one of the company's employees. I heard from another employee that the man used to work for a company that burned to the ground a few years ago in Houston."

"Sure, what's the employee's name?"

"Quincy Cummings," Darius said, hoping Walt would be able to obtain information about the guy.

"I'll let you know something in a day or so," Walt said.

"Thanks, I appreciate it."

"So, what's been going on with you, Darius? The last time we talked was over a year ago. I thought you were calling to let me know you had gotten married or something," Walt said in a joking tone. But for some reason Darius was annoyed by Walt's words—they had definitely hit a nerve. It could be because Walt had been the one to tell him about Summer and the things she had said about him.

"Not hardly. I plan to stay single for the rest of my days," Darius said, wondering why each and every time he talked to Walt, his marital status came up.

"Same here, man. Women are nothing but liars. None of them can be trusted. Hey, remember that good-looking broad you had the hots for when we were partners? The one who dumped you for some rich old man when you were out of town? I don't recall her name but I—"

"Summer," Darius cut in, trying to keep his tone from showing the irritation he felt.

"What?"

"I said her name was Summer. Summer Martindale," Darius said, ready to end the call.

"Oh, yeah, that's right. I wonder what happened to her after she left Houston. If she and that old man she ran off with are still together."

"I wouldn't know," Darius said shortly, deciding not to mention that Summer was now living in Somerset and he had not only run into her but had kissed her again. "Look, Walt. I appreciate you calling me back. Let me know if you find something out on that employee."

"Sure thing, pal."

Darius hung up the phone. Walt was the kind of man who believed misery loved company and had always seemed miserable, mainly because he'd had a tough time when it came to women.

Deciding he needed that file he'd left back at the shelter, he made a turn at the next traffic light. A few moments later, he was pulling into the parking lot and was surprised to see Summer's car in the usual spot. Why was she still here?

It didn't take him long to get out of his car and walk toward the shelter's entrance. The security guy named Barney recognized him but followed security procedures before allowing him entry.

"Is Ms. Martindale in her office?" he asked the man as he stuffed his ID back into his wallet.

"Yes, sir, and I did as you asked and walked her to her car last night."

"Thanks. I appreciate it."

Walking toward Summer's office, he stopped at the night-duty secretary's station. He had met the older woman, Raycine Bradley, the evening before. "Good evening, Ms. Bradley, is Ms. Martindale meeting with someone?" he asked.

The woman smiled at him. "No. I think she's packing up to call it a night. Finally."

Darius nodded, thinking Summer should have done that long ago. "I think I'll go hurry her along," he said, heading to the corridor that led to Summer's office.

Moments later he knocked on her door.

"Come in."

He stepped into her office and closed the door behind him. She was standing at a table with her back to him sorting out papers. Without looking his way, she said, "I promise I'll be leaving in a few minutes, Raycine."

Darius crossed his arms over his chest and leaned against the closed door. "That's good to hear. I intend to do everything in my power to make sure that you do."

Summer swirled around and stared at Darius in surprise. From the look on his face, he wasn't a happy camper. "What are you doing here?" she asked.

"I need to ask you that same thing," he said in a curt tone, moving away from the door to stand in the middle of her office with his hands braced on his hips.

Now she knew what had him upset. He didn't like the fact she was still there. She couldn't help wondering why he was making it his business. "I had a lot to do for tomorrow's meeting with Mr. Novak. In addition to that, a new woman checked into our facilities today."

She saw the look of concern that immediately showed on his face. "How is she?"

"She was a lot better once we got her settled in and assured her that if her husband showed up here, we wouldn't let him near her."

Darius shook his head. "It's sad that any woman has to worry about something like that."

Summer sighed deeply. "Yes. Been there. Done that."

But she didn't have to remind him of that since he'd been a part of that particular drama in her past. She had truly believed a restraining order would keep Tyrone away from her. He had proven her wrong. She didn't want to think about what might have happened if Darius hadn't shown up when he did, putting his life on the line for her.

Not wanting to think about Tyrone any longer, she asked, "So, are you going to tell me why you're here?" His gaze stroked her like a physical caress she couldn't ignore.

"I left something I need for tomorrow. I forgot to mention that I won't be back here until next week, when I start setting up the billing account."

"Oh." She should have been thrilled that she wouldn't be seeing him for the fourth day in a row but a barrage of emotions she couldn't explain tried to engulf her. She fought them back.

"I'm working on a case that requires my attention elsewhere," he added.

She wanted to tell him that he owed her no explanation. Instead, she said, "Sounds real serious."

"It's a case involving arson. You probably read about it in the papers a few weeks back. A fire at the Brody Oil and Gas refinery."

"Yes, I do recall reading about it," she said, leaning against the table. "And you think it was deliberately set?"

"It looks that way. I've been asked by the Brody brothers to find out who did it."

Summer eyed Darius. She recalled how much he'd enjoyed his job as a detective. Once in a while he would tell her about a particular case he was trying to solve. "Got any leads?" she asked.

"Not enough to suit me, which is the reason I need to spend a day at the refinery." He moved over toward her. "So, what do you need me to do?"

She straightened her stance. "About what?"

"About helping you pack up and get out of here, like you should have done hours ago."

"I told you why I'm still here."

"But your reason isn't good enough. I can see you staying over for an hour or so, but damn it Summer, it's going on eleven o'clock and knowing you, you'll be back here first thing in the morning."

"Of course. My meeting is at eight."

Darius wondered how she would feel knowing he had just finished playing a game of pool with the man she would be meeting with. And now Kev knew she was someone from his past, someone who had once meant a lot to him. His friend knew how much she had hurt him, as well. "So, what can I do to help?" he asked.

When Darius came to a stop in front of her, Summer released a resigned sigh. It wouldn't do any good to argue with him. Besides, she was too tired. "I guess you can help by stapling these papers that I've already sorted."

"Okay."

She tried to scoot over when he joined her at the table but their arms touched nonetheless, and she felt it—a spark of sensations that swept through her. She inhaled a sharp breath.

He glanced over at her. "You're all right?"

She breathed in deeply before saying, "Yes, I'm fine. Why wouldn't I be?"

"No reason."

There was a reason and they both knew it. Memories filtered through her mind of a night she just couldn't forget. There was no way she could deny that over the years she had lain in bed missing a warm, hard body beside her, and being awakened by the taste of a desire so potent it could blind you.

"If you're meeting just with Kevin Novak, why are you making all of these handouts?"

His question cut into her thoughts and she glanced over at him. "For the other members of the TCC, for him to share with them. I want everyone to know what's going on here at the shelter, that we're benefiting the community and that I'm competent enough to handle things."

Darius reached out and touched her arm. "You're worried for nothing. If they thought you weren't competent enough to handle things, you wouldn't be here."

"But what if—"

He reached for her. "For crying out loud, woman, you worry too much."

She should have seen it coming and backed away from him. But the moment his mouth touched hers she knew she could not have moved an inch. And now that her stomach was contracting with desire, there was no way she wasn't going to enjoy it while it lasted.

That was one thing she was truthful about, the fact that Darius knew how to kiss, even during those times when he should be doing something else. Like now. He had offered to help her, not seduce her. Awareness, bold and daring, raced through her, made her acknowledge that Darius was the only man who could ever make her purr in his arms. The only man who'd made her feel she'd been cheated out of many more nights with him.

*If only...*

She didn't want to think about if only. She only wanted to think about now, not what did or didn't happen seven years ago and during the years in between. She didn't even want to think about why being in his arms felt natural, like a place she should be. A place she belonged. His mouth felt in sync with hers, also totally natural, connected to hers while kissing her so perfectly.

When he finally ended the kiss, she couldn't do anything but pull in a deep breath, still tasting him on her lips. She didn't bother giving herself a mental shake and questioning why she had let him kiss her. She knew very well why. She wouldn't do as she'd done the last time, pretending she hadn't wanted any part of it since, like before, she hadn't resisted. She doubted that she could have even if she'd wanted to.

But she didn't want to talk about it. Without saying anything, she turned back to the table and gathered up what was left of the papers she had sorted. She was fully aware that he was watching her, but following her lead, he didn't say anything, either. Out of the corner of her eye, she could see him neatly stacking the handouts she'd made. They turned at the same time and their gazes locked for a mere second before simultaneously, they stepped into each other's arms again.

It seemed what was happening at the moment was Summer's mind was refusing to remember the bad times, only the good. And there had been good times, as good as good could get. They had only shared a bed once but before then, they had shared companionship, although she'd found out later he'd had an ulterior motive for doing so. But she wouldn't dwell on that now. The only thing she wanted to dwell on was the way his mouth was taking hers, with a hunger she could feel all the way to her toes, with an intensity that had her stomach churning as they were enjoying this kiss to the fullest.

It didn't even bother her that he was holding her

in a possessive and intimate way, with his hands cradling her backside to fit her pelvis snugly against the front of him. She could feel the muscled tone of his body and his erection, hard and strong, pressed against her.

Taking his cue, she wrapped her arms around his neck as he sank deeper into her mouth, sending points of pleasure all through her. She felt sensations in her fingers as she caressed the back part of his neck, and through the material of her skirt where she was making contact with his denim-clad thigh. And she was very well aware of when he changed the angle of his mouth to position hers more to his advantage.

His efforts had her mind reeling, filling her with an urgent need to recognize and accept what was taking place, giving her the resolve to simply stand there, indulge and take it like a woman. And she was. She was taking it like a woman who needed every stroke of his tongue, every bit of his taste and every mind-blowing, tantalizing sensation his mouth was making her feel.

When the kiss ended moments later, she couldn't resist placing a lingering heated kiss on his jawline. Nor could she resist taking the tip of her tongue and tracing along his upper lip before finally taking a step back.

Darius drew in a deep breath and fought the urge to pull her back into his arms again, ask if he could follow her home and make love to her with the same intensity that he had made love to her that night. But this time, his heart wouldn't come into play, only his lust.

He wished the kiss could have wiped away all the wrongs of the past and he could move on without feeling animosity in his heart. Unfortunately, it hadn't. What it had done was make him fully aware of how vulnerable his heart still was when it came to Summer, and just how hot and strong his desire for her still burned within every part of his body.

"Finish up in here so I can walk you to your car," he heard himself say in a deep, throaty voice. A yearning for her was stirring his insides, thundering all the way through his veins, making him want to say the hell with it and take her on that very table.

But he couldn't. He wouldn't.

"I'll be fine, Darius. I don't need you to walk me to my car."

As he studied her, he saw the way her eyes glowed in a seductive lure. He doubted she even realized it. He needed to act accordingly and not give in to what she was asking for without even knowing she was doing so.

"I'm walking you out anyway, Summer."

He saw the lure in her eyes quicken to a sharp edge and he wouldn't be surprised if she stood her ground. Then it would become a standoff, since he had every intention of walking her out. In fact, he intended to follow her home to make sure she got inside her house safely.

"Fine. Suit yourself, Darius."

Her words ripped through the air. He could tell by her tone that she wasn't happy, but that didn't bother him. When it came to her safety there was no compromising. He moved from the table to stand in front of her desk, convincing himself that it was his protective instincts kicking in where she was concerned, and nothing more.

Darius watched as Summer grabbed her purse and then he followed her out the door, pausing in the hall while she locked up her office. The shelter was quiet since most of the people in residence were probably in bed, asleep. "What did you have for dinner?" he asked when they began walking down the corridor toward the lobby.

"I worked through dinner."

Darius pressed his lips together to keep from saying a word that might have burned her ears. Knowing she had missed a meal bothered him a lot more than he cared to admit.

"And please, Darius, no sermons. I'm too beat to listen."

He glanced over at her. "I don't do sermons."

"Could have fooled me."

He halted his steps and brought her to a stop before rounding the corner that led to the lobby. She might be too beat to listen to what he had to say, but there was no doubt in his mind that she had plenty of energy for an argument and was gearing up for one. However, he had no intention of obliging her.

He leaned forward and placed a light kiss on her

lips. "You're much prettier when you're not trying to be difficult."

She frowned up at him, clearly caught off guard. "I'm not trying to be difficult."

He couldn't help but smile. "Could have fooled me."

He didn't even try to hold back a chuckle when she narrowed her gaze at him. Ignoring the look, his hand took hold of her elbow. "Come on, Summer, let me grab that file off my desk and then get you home before you fall flat on your face from exhaustion."

Summer glanced over her shoulder before opening the door to her house. She had been fully aware that Darius had followed her home. She could have been nice and invited him in, but she'd decided not to. There was only so much Darius Franklin she could take, and after the kisses they'd shared in her office tonight, she had reached her limit for today.

She didn't have to wonder what there was about him that made her feel so raw and exposed yet at the same time so well protected. Whenever they kissed, she couldn't help but recall the passion. And then there were the memories of the hopes and dreams that had blossomed in her heart of what she'd assumed was a promising future between them. She had even allowed her dreams to include marriage and babies.

She headed for the bathroom to take her shower, wondering if at any time during the past seven years Darius had regretted bragging about their night together in such a degrading manner to his partner, Walt Stewart. She appreciated the fact that Walt felt she needed to know just what Darius had said.

Pain tore into her heart every time she realized just how wrong she had been about him, and that made her determined not to make another mistake by giving him her heart a second time. But she *had* enjoyed their kiss. In her mind, one didn't have to do with the other, just as long as she knew where she stood with him and where he stood with her.

He was now a dedicated businessman who seemed to enjoy what he did for a living and she had a new life, a new career and was no longer looking over her shoulder, fearful of seeing Tyrone. The past seven years had been good for her, although lonely. When it came to men she had learned the hard way to play it safe, and she would continue to do so.

And one sure way to do that was to make sure she didn't assume anything where Darius was concerned.

Darius needed a shower to relax. After making sure Summer had gotten home okay, he had driven straight home with memories of their kisses running all through his mind. Having her in his arms had felt natural, like that was where she belonged. Considering what she'd done to him seven years ago, was that weird or what?

When he had reluctantly ended their kiss, she had taken her tongue and swept it across his lips. He still felt a stirring deep in his gut just thinking about it. It had been unexpected. It had felt good.

And now he knew where she lived and would make it his business to get her to invite him over to her place one night. It might take a while to work up to that, but he would get there. He wouldn't see her again until Monday, which was just as well since he of all people knew Summer was the type of woman who could grow on a man.

She was the type of woman who could easily get under a man's skin. And he had to admit that she had gotten under his tonight. She had made sensations he hadn't felt in years rush through him, reminding him what it was like to lose control with a woman.

Darius headed toward the shower with a deep frown on his face. No matter what Summer evoked within him, he was determined to remain immune to her charms. He had no intentions of making the same mistake twice.

# Six

"How did your meeting go on Friday?"

Summer glanced up and met Darius's gaze. She had wondered if he would be dropping by the shelter today. She hadn't expected to see him Friday, but she hadn't known for sure when he would be back to complete the project he'd been hired by the TCC to do.

"I think the meeting went great. Mr. Novak appreciated the handouts and was very attentive to what I had to say. He agreed that based on our occupancy log, it would be a good idea to consider expanding the facilities sooner than later. He said he'd take his recommendations back to the other members of the TCC."

Darius nodded. "And how was your weekend?"

"Busy as usual. And yours?" she asked, watching

him carefully. She used to have the ability to read his thoughts, but now his expressions were unrevealing and she didn't have a clue as to what he was thinking.

"It was okay. After spending Friday at the refinery, I had to follow up several leads," he said, stepping into the room.

She immediately felt his heat, breathed in his scent and admitted to herself that she had missed seeing him around. "And you're still certain the fire was intentionally set?"

She tried not to notice how good he looked standing in front of her desk with a cup of coffee in his hand. All it took was a glance at his mouth to remember their kisses right here in this office last week.

She refused to admit she had purposely left her office door open on the off chance he dropped by Helping Hands today. On a number of occasions he had caught her unaware and she didn't want that to happen this time. She also refused to admit that she had thought about him a lot over the weekend, wondering how he was spending his time—and with whom. The latter was something she had no right to concern herself with, but she couldn't help it.

"I'll pick up the official report from the fire marshal this week, but so far, all evidence still points to arson," he said.

"Then I'm sure you'll be the one to solve this case."

Darius didn't want to think about what effect her confidence had on him at that very moment. She'd always had a way of making him feel that he could leap tall buildings with a single bound if he had to. He used to tell himself the reason she felt that way was because he had been the one to save her from a dangerous situation, and he shouldn't put much stock into it. But he had anyway.

"So, what's next?"

That was another thing that had drawn him to Summer, her interest in his job. She would ask questions and seemed to understand his excitement about it as well as his frustrations. He would enjoy getting off work at the end of his shift and dropping by her place to tell her how his day had gone.

"I'll continue to conduct an investigation over at the refinery while working on the security and the accounting systems here. Since the TCC wants me to personally handle both, I've delegated my other projects."

There, he'd just told her his plans which meant, whether she liked it or not, he would be hanging around for a while. He wondered if she had assumed he would be moving on and assigning the shelter job to someone else, but he couldn't read her expression.

"Well, I'll let you get back to work. I'll see you at noon."

He watched as her brow lifted. "Noon?"

He smiled. "Yes. We're doing lunch."

She stared at him. "Are we?"

"Sure we are, and I'll even let you twist my arm into getting one of those salads you seem to like so much."

There was a pause, and Darius sensed she was trying to determine whether it was worth the effort to start an argument with him. When she began speaking, she spoke her words slowly as if to make sure they were understood. "I don't want you to assume we're going to lunch together every day, Darius."

"Don't you like my company?"

She hesitated, and he watched her nervously lick her top lip with her tongue before she answered. "Whether I like your company or not has nothing to do with it. We have issues we haven't yet resolved."

They had issues yet to be resolved? She made it sound like she had been the injured party and not the other way around. He hadn't been the one to skip town with a man old enough to be her father who could buy her all the things Darius couldn't afford on his detective salary. They would resolve things all right, but his way. Pretty soon she would see how it felt to have someone you assumed loved you turn around and leave you high and dry with a broken heart.

"Some things can't be resolved and are better left alone," he said. "And in our case, maybe that's the way things should be, Summer. What happened between us was seven years ago. People change and they grow to regret things they did when they were young and foolish."

Darius maintained eye contact with her, assuming she was thinking about what he'd said. He made it sound as if he was giving her a chance to redeem herself, and that he was willing to forgive her for what she had done. Little did she know how far from the truth that was.

"Maybe you have the right idea," she finally said. "It *was* seven years ago and we've grown a lot since then."

"I'd like to believe we have." Deciding he didn't want to discuss it any further, he asked, "So, do we have another date for lunch?"

She hesitated and then said, "Yes, we do."

After Darius walked out of her office, Summer couldn't help wondering if she was making a mistake by agreeing to put the past behind them. He evidently found it easy to do so, but he hadn't been the one to get his heart broken. But then, on the other hand, she couldn't discount the fact that Darius had saved her life. And then another part of her wondered if perhaps she had put more stock in their affair, and had expected more from the relationship than he had.

She had gone a long time without getting involved with a man and she wasn't so sure if she could handle Darius—she wasn't even sure if she wanted to. She had gotten used to being by herself. Why was he determined to invade her space?

The only thing she was certain about was the way he made her feel whenever he touched her. To be honest, he didn't even have to touch her to make her hormones react. He could stand five feet away and she had the ability to feel how the tension in the air surrounding them seemed to vibrate, emitting all sorts of sensuous stirrings and longings. He had been in her office less than fifteen minutes and already her vital signs were at their highest peak.

But she was no longer concerned by the staggering degree of physical chemistry flowing between them. It had always been there, from the first. What she was concerned about was how easily she wanted to forgive him and believe that what Darius had said was true. Seven years ago, they had been different people with different values, at a different place in their lives. People change. And they come to regret decisions and actions of their past. Decisions and actions that they can't change.

She knew some men didn't like confrontation and Darius was probably of the mind that even if they hashed the issues out, it would not change anything. But still, was it too much to expect an apology for sharing something private and personal with his partner? Couldn't he see that doing so had degraded what they'd shared?

Even now she could vividly recall that day, after she and Darius had spent the night together. He had left her bed that morning seemingly in a good mood, making plans for them to spend the day together. But first he had to go home to get a change of clothes and stop by police headquarters to complete some paperwork, and she had to work a few hours at the restaurant where she was a part-time waitress.

When she'd returned home, she had waited for Darius. When hours passed, she had gotten worried. That evening, Walt had appeared on her doorstep with a message from Darius saying he'd had to leave town unexpectedly on police business. After delivering that message, Walt had asked if he could talk to her privately. That is when he'd told her how Darius had come to the station that day and bragged about finally sleeping with her. He had made a bet with Walt that it would take less than a month to share her bed. Discovering their one night together hadn't been anything more than a chance for him to win a bet had hurt her deeply. And then to know he'd gone back and told his friend had been another crushing blow.

While listening to Walt level with her about what Darius had done, she had barely been able to maintain her composure. Only after Walt had left did she break down and let it all out. She knew she had to leave Houston immediately and did not want to see Darius again, ever. It had been bad enough with Tyrone, but the hurt Darius had inflicted was even worse because in just a short time, she had fallen in love with him.

She had been too ashamed to call her aunt to tell her what had happened, so in the days that followed, she'd made some quick decisions. One of her regular customers at the restaurant, an author of academic books named Jack Lindsey, would be spending a year in Florida with his wife while he penned his next book. Jack had offered her the chance to accompany them as his assistant, to organize and edit all of his notes. He had made the offer before, but she had turned him down because of Tyrone's threats regarding what he would do if she ever left town. But with no future for her in Houston, she had quickly packed up and left town with the Lindseys.

The Lindseys had been wonderful and she had enjoyed the year she had spent with them on their beach property in Miami. She had buried herself in her work, determined to put Darius out of her mind and go about healing her heart. When she hadn't heard from him in over two weeks, that had only verified everything Walt had said. Their night together had been a conquest for him and nothing more.

Since both Mr. and Mrs. Lindsey were former teachers, they had encouraged Summer to pursue a college degree, and Mrs. Lindsey had even tutored her on those subjects Summer had felt would hold her back from getting accepted to any college. Using the money she'd made working for the Lindseys, along with a very nice bonus they had given her at the end of the year, she had remained in Miami to attend college there. She had poured all her time and energy into her classes, determined to reach every goal she had established for herself and refusing to wallow in the hurt and pain Darius had caused her.

Summer got up from her desk and looked out the window, not sure how she would handle the one man she thought she would never see again.

What she was up against now was how he could make her feel. Whenever she was around him, he was capable of bringing out feelings and desires that she wished would stay buried. In seven years, no man had made her remember how it felt to be a woman. A desired woman. It was something Darius could do so effortlessly.

When he met her gaze, she could see the desire in his eyes, and on most occasions he wasn't trying to mask it. It was as if he knew exactly what he was doing to her, what buttons to push, what words to say.

She had thought about him a lot over the weekend, wondering how and what he was doing. And, she thought as she bit her lower lip, with whom. She wished she could claim she didn't care, but she did. She couldn't help but notice how ladies would glance their way whenever they walked into the café together. There was feminine interest in their eyes and she couldn't very well blame them for it. After all, she was a woman, too.

She sighed deeply before checking her watch. It was time to make her rounds and greet everyone. She would keep herself busy until lunchtime.

Darius stared long and hard at the computer screen, thinking he must have missed something while setting up the billing system. He needed to go back and recheck. Or better yet, he thought, leaning back in the chair and rubbing the bridge of his nose, it would probably be a good idea if he kept his mind on what he was doing and stopped thinking about Summer. Having her on his mind was probably the reason he'd thought he'd found a number of irregularities in the TCC's accounting.

Deciding to give both his eyes and his mind a break, he pushed away from the desk and stood, needing to stretch his body. He had been sitting at the computer practically all morning and the limited space under the desk had been murder on his long legs.

He glanced at his watch. He had another hour to go before lunch and he couldn't deny he was looking forward to dining with Summer again. He tried convincing himself that spending time with her meant absolutely nothing, and was just a part of his plan for revenge. There was no reason to think it was anything more than that.

He breathed in deeply, truly wishing he believed that. But he knew if he wasn't careful, he would be succumbing to Summer's charms all over again. And he didn't want that. He had given his heart to her once and what she'd done had almost destroyed him, made him unable to put his complete trust in another woman.

He had asked her how her meeting with Kev had gone, but he'd already been privy to that information. To say she had impressed Kev was an understatement. Besides stating the obvious about what a good-looking woman she was, Kev had been taken with her keen sense of intelligence as well as her concern for the women who sought refuge at the shelter. Kev also felt she had a lot of good ideas that the TCC should definitely take under consideration.

Sitting back down at the computer, he resumed setting up the Helping Hands account, trying to push thoughts of Summer to the back of his mind. However, once again a few discrepancies within TCC's accounting system popped up.

He pulled back when his cell phone went off. It was Lance. "Yeah, Lance, what's up?"

"Kate's fixing dinner tonight and wants you to come eat with us."

Darius smiled. He liked Kate and would be the first to say she was just what Lance needed. "I'd love to."

"Great. I'll let her know."

"Lance?"

"Yeah?"

Darius paused, not sure if he should mention anything about the discrepancies he'd found in TCC's accounting. Huntington and his band of tight-wads managed the accounting for the club—namely the money they got from fundraisers and endowments. And everybody knew his group kept a tight squeeze on TCC's money supply. If there was anything wrong with the club's funds, they would know it. But still…

"Darius? What is it?"

Darius breathed in deeply. "Nothing," he finally said, deciding not to jump to any conclusions about the discrepancies until he'd had a chance to look at them more carefully.

"How are things going with you and Summer Martindale?"

Darius frowned. "You talk as if we're a couple."

"Aren't you?" Lance countered.

"Not yet."

There must have been something in his voice that gave him away.

"I don't know what your plans are regarding her, Darius, but be careful. They can backfire on you. If you're going to pursue her, then you need to forget about what happened seven years ago and move on."

Darius didn't say anything for a moment and then admitted, "I can't."

"You should try, man. When the shit blows up in your face, don't say I didn't warn you."

"Today I came prepared," Darius said, glancing down at his feet.

Summer followed his gaze and noted he had removed his boots and was now wearing a pair of leather loafers. That meant he had come to the shelter today prepared to walk over to the café, and *had* assumed she would have lunch with him. She wasn't sure whether she liked the fact that he'd known she would give in.

She returned her gaze to his face. "So I see. You're ready?"

"I'm always ready, Summer."

She had absolute confidence in the truth of that statement. "Excuse me for a second. I need to let Marcy know I'm leaving."

She walked over to Marcy's desk. Marcy was in her late fifties and was someone Summer had become close to since working at the shelter. "I'm going to lunch now, Marcy."

Marcy smiled. "Okay. Did you ever get that dripping faucet at your house fixed?"

Summer shook her head. "Not yet, but I better do so soon, since it's keeping me from getting a good night's sleep." She then turned to rejoin Darius and together they left the building to walk over to the café for lunch. Her morning had been busy and she needed time away from the shelter. She always enjoyed her lunch, at least whenever she could make time for it.

It was a beautiful day and for some reason, Summer couldn't push aside the pleasurable sensations she was feeling with Darius beside her. She felt lucky today. She had counseled two women that morning and after listening to their stories, a part of her felt blessed that she had cut her ties with Tyrone when she had, otherwise she could have been one of them. And although Tyrone had caused unnecessary drama that had landed him behind bars for twenty years, she was free to make choices about her life. Now it was her job to convince those two women they could make choices about their lives, as well.

"So, how has your day been so far?" Darius asked.

She began sharing bits and pieces of how busy she'd been as they continued their walk to the café. Although his legs were a lot longer than hers, he adjusted his steps to keep in line with hers. More than once, while sharing her ideas about a number of things she would like to see happen at the shelter, she would glance up and see how absorbed he was in what she was saying. They were ideas she hadn't shared with Kevin Novak for not wanting to overwhelm the man since everything she had in mind included a hefty price tag. But they were expenditures she felt would greatly benefit the women who sought refuge at the shelter.

Then, while it was on her mind, she asked about his brother, something she should have done long before now since she knew how close the two of them were. Like her, he had lost his parents at an early age, and he and his brother had been raised by their grandmother.

"Ethan is doing fine now."

She opened her mouth to ask what he meant by that when suddenly a warm, masculine arm snaked around her waist to stop her from stepping in a rut in the cement sidewalk. "Thank you."

"Don't mention it," he said, releasing her.

Summer tried to ignore the sensations that raced through her veins at his touch. When they reached the café and he opened the door, she quickly moved past him, wondering how she was going to get through her meal.

Kate Thornton Brody smiled up at Darius. "You need a woman in your life," she said.

Darius lifted a brow, wondering where that had come from. He glanced across the living room and shot Lance a questioning look, but all his friend did was smile and shrug his shoulders. Damn, he hadn't been in the house five minutes and already Kate was on him about being single.

Seeing that Lance wouldn't be giving him much help, Darius reached out and placed a friendly arm around Kate's shoulder. "Sweetheart, you know I prefer being single."

She gave him one of her sidelong looks that said

she'd taken what he'd said with a grain of salt. "So did Lance at one time."

"But now he has you and he's a lucky man," Darius said truthfully. He had known Kate ever since she began working for Lance as his very competent administrative assistant when he took over Brody Oil and Gas a few years back, and had always liked her.

"What's for dinner? I'm starving," he quickly said, before Kate could make another comment about the state of his affairs or lack of them.

"Didn't you eat lunch?" Lance asked, finally moving off the sofa.

Lance's question reminded him of Summer…not that he could forget. He hated admitting that whenever he had lunch with her, it was a pleasant experience. She was a great conversationalist. Always had been. And today she'd seemed more relaxed with him, more at ease. And as usual, she had looked beautiful sitting across from him.

"Yes, I had lunch," he finally said. "A salad."

Humor lit Lance's eyes. "A salad? What kind of foolishness is that?"

"Don't let Lance tease you, Darius. There's nothing wrong with eating a salad," Kate said, walking back toward the kitchen.

When she was gone, Lance looked at him and chuckled. "I take it you had lunch with Summer."

Darius met Lance's amused look. "What makes you think that?"

"She's the salad girl."

Darius couldn't help but smile. When he'd left Houston because of Ethan's accident, Lance had shown up in Charleston to give him the support he needed. It was during that time that he had told Lance all about Summer, even how much she liked eating salads.

"I'd like to meet her. Invite her over one—"

"It's not that kind of relationship, Lance, and you know it," he said quickly, deciding to squash any foolish ideas that might be floating around in his best friend's head.

"Whatever you say," Lance said, smiling.

"I'm serious, Lance."

"Of course you are. I believe you."

Darius frowned. He could tell his friend really didn't believe him. "It's hard to love someone who has hurt you deeply," he said.

The amusement disappeared from Lance's face. "I'm glad everyone doesn't feel that way, Darius, or I wouldn't have Kate as my wife. If you recall, I almost lost her when I announced my engagement to another woman. But she still found it in her heart to give me another chance."

Darius's frown deepened. "So, what are you trying to say?"

Lance held his friend's gaze. "What I'm trying to say is that if you love someone, there can always be forgiveness."

"I really appreciate you walking me out to my car again, Barney, but it's really not necessary," Summer said to the security guard at her side.

"No problem, Ms. Martindale. Besides, it's Mr. Franklin's orders."

Summer shook her head, still not sure how Darius could give orders when he wasn't paying the man's salary. She was just about to ask Barney how that was possible when he suddenly said, "Someone has slashed your tires."

"What?"

"Your tires," he said, pointing his flashlight on her car. "They've been slashed."

Summer followed the beam of light and saw what he was talking about. She hauled in a deep breath, recalling the last time her tires had been slashed and who had been responsible. She forced herself to calm down as old fears tried to resurface.

That was all seven years ago. Tyrone was locked up and couldn't touch her. More than likely, the husband or significant other of one of the women at the shelter was venting his anger on her since the shelter was standing in the way of the person he really wanted to take it out on. But it couldn't be Samuel Green, since he was still locked up, held without bond.

"I need to follow procedures and report this to the police, Ms. Martindale," Barney was saying, interrupting her thoughts. "Please come back inside while I contact the authorities and complete an incident report."

Summer turned her attention away from her tires. "Yes, of course."

She moved to follow him back inside. She'd heard

reports of acts of revenge being directed at staff members who work with victims of violence. Incidents of rock throwing, drive-by shootings and even bomb threats had been reported. As far as she was concerned, the person who damaged her tires was nothing but a bully.

"Are you all right, Ms. Martindale?" Barney asked with concern when they had reached the door to go back inside.

She forced a smile on her lips. "Yes, I'm fine." She heard the words she'd just spoken, but wasn't sure she believed them herself.

# Seven

"What's this about your tires getting slashed last night?"

Summer glanced up and saw Darius leaning in her office doorway. News had spread quickly. The evening crew from last night had a lot to share with the staffers that had arrived that morning. She'd figured he would hear about the incident sooner or later. She wished it had been later, since she really didn't want to talk about it right now.

"I'm sure you've heard the story, Darius, and I'm not in the mood to rehash it."

"Humor me," he said, crossing the threshold and closing the door behind him. She couldn't help but study his features. There was something different about his eyes. Their darkness was still striking, but now they contained an element of hardness she hadn't seen since that first day he had discovered her working at the shelter. And his lips were pressed together in a tight line. On most days, it wouldn't take much to look at his lips and remember how they had introduced her to pleasures of the most decadent kind in a single night.

"I'm listening."

Summer blinked. While she had been staring at him, probably like a lust-crazed woman, he had taken a seat in the chair in front of her desk. She leaned back, trying to relax under the intensity of his direct gaze, but found it difficult to do so.

"What you've already heard is probably correct," she started. "Barney walked me out to the car like he's been doing since that incident with Samuel Green and noticed my tires had been slashed. We came back inside, called the police to report it and he filled out an incident report. End of story."

"I don't think so."

She heard the near growl in his voice. He was angry, she could tell. And she knew his anger was not directed at her but at whomever had slashed her tires. Given his mood, that was a comforting thought.

"I want to find out who did it," he said in the same tone of voice. "What did the police say?"

She shrugged. "Not much. They would have liked a list of the women residing here to check out the names of husbands and boyfriends, but because of our confidentiality policy, we couldn't provide it for them. I contacted the TCC earlier today to see if we could have two guards here at night instead of one."

"I thought there were two guards here since the night of that incident with Green."

"That lasted all but two days before one of them was pulled. Evidently, the TCC rehashed the idea and felt only one was needed. That's why I called them—to see if they would reconsider since the staff members around here were beginning to get nervous. However, the man I spoke with at the TCC said adding an additional guard wasn't going to happen."

"Who did you talk to?"

"I asked for Kevin Novak but the person I talked to was an older gentleman by the name of Sebastian Huntington." She saw his jaw twitch. "You know him."

"Yes, I know him."

Summer noticed that he'd said the words in a tight voice with more than a little distaste. "He wasn't very friendly," she added. "Nothing at all like Mr. Novak."

He didn't say anything but from the way he was looking at her, she knew he was taking it all in. And then he asked, "Is there anything else?"

She shook her head. "No, nothing other than the piece of paper that had been placed on my car, which I also mentioned to the police last night."

He lifted a brow, his posture on full alert. "What paper?"

"One night last week someone placed a note under the wiper blade. Barney had walked me to my car, and he pulled it off and gave it to me, thinking it was some kind of sales flyer. It wasn't until I stopped at a traffic light and glanced at it did I notice what it said."

"And what did it say?" he asked, leaning closer and moving toward the edge of his seat.

She swallowed, remembering precisely what was written in bold letters on the paper. "It said, 'I take care of my own.'"

The moment Darius left Summer's office he darted into an empty conference room and called Kevin. He picked up on the second ring. "This is Kevin."

"Kev, were you informed that Huntington had reduced the number of security guards at Helping Hands?"

"No."

An angry Darius went on to tell Kevin about the incident that had occurred last night.

"Huntington has no right to make those kinds of decisions without discussing it with the committee first, and I am part of that committee," Kevin said, almost livid.

"The man's been a part of the TCC for so long I believe he thinks he owns it, which is why he constantly overlooks anything the younger members have to say," Darius said.

"And how is Summer Martindale?"

"She's a little shaken up, although she was trying not to show it. The staff here is nervous—first Green breaking doors down and now this tire-slashing incident.

It doesn't bode well. There have been revenge-type incidents reported in various cities around the country, and they are aware of it. We need to make sure they feel protected."

Darius tried to convince himself that his concern for Summer was no different than his concern for any other woman he'd once been involved with, but deep down a part of him knew that wasn't true. He would even go so far as to admit missing her whenever he spent time away from Helping Hands.

They were feelings that he didn't want to feel. One way to remedy that was to start keeping his distance, but then he wouldn't be able to make her feel the way he had felt when she'd left. He just needed to make sure he kept things in perspective.

"I totally agree," Kevin said, bringing Darius's attention back to the matter at hand. "I'll confront Huntington myself, and if I have to, I'll call a special meeting of the board."

Moments later, Darius hung up the phone feeling a lot better than he had before making the call to Kev. He knew his friend wouldn't like the "executive" decision Huntington had made regarding the security at the shelter any more than he did. As usual, the man was trying to throw his weight around, fighting for power he really didn't have. But Darius relaxed a bit, knowing Kev was on it.

He glanced at his watch. He needed to leave for a while to attend to business concerning the fire at the refinery—he had to talk to several guys who had been off work the day he'd met with the employees the last time. But he intended to return to the shelter before Summer left for lunch. The thought of her walking anywhere alone troubled his mind.

From now on, he would make sure that she was well protected. At all costs.

Three days later, Summer glanced over at Darius before looking down at her watch. It was a little past eight in the evening. She had volunteered to stay for a few hours to help man the abuse hotline, and he had surprised her when he volunteered to assist her.

At first, she hadn't been sure whether women on the other line would want to unload their pain and anguish to a man, but from overhearing bits and pieces of his conversations, she could tell he was handling things quite nicely. She would be the first to admit that he had a good demeanor for assisting those who called in, male or female.

"What time are you leaving?" she asked him. Since the night her tires had gotten slashed, he had made it his business to return to the shelter every day after being at the refinery in the mornings, to walk her to the café for lunch. And if she remained late in the evenings, he did so, as well. Then he would not only walk her to her car, but would follow her home to make sure she got in safely.

"I'll leave when you leave," he said, glancing over at her.

In a way, his protectiveness irked her. She didn't

want him to feel like she needed him in any way. "There are two security guards now, so I'll be all right." She really hadn't been surprised when, the day after the tire-slashing incident, two guards were on duty. There was no doubt in her mind that Darius had had something to do with it, although what exactly, she wasn't sure.

"I plan to leave in a few minutes," she said.

He smiled over at her. "Then so will I."

And he did. After she had handled the last call she would take, she gathered up her belongings and headed for the door with him by her side. He nodded to the guards on duty as they passed.

"Nice night," he said.

She looked up at the sky and saw the full moon and the stars, and how they illuminated the otherwise dark sky. He was right. It was a nice night.

"I'll be following you home again."

She glanced over at him. "It's your gas."

She said nothing as they continued walking. When he opened the car door for her, she slid inside, noticing how his gaze shifted to her legs when her skirt accidentally showed a little bit of flesh. She started to say something about his wandering eyes and decided not to. It probably wouldn't do any good anyway.

The drive to her place was uneventful and whenever she glanced in her rearview mirror, he was there. She would admit that, considering the incidents of the past two weeks, she felt a semblance of security knowing he was near, just like the days and nights following that episode with Tyrone.

She parked her car in the driveway and was surprised when he parked behind her and got out of his vehicle. The other times he had followed her home, he had stayed in the car while she went inside and then left. She wondered why he had changed the routine, and she didn't like the way her skin seemed to feel warm all over as he came closer.

"You have a two-car garage. Any reason you aren't parking in it?" he asked, coming to a stop in front of her.

"It's full of boxes. I haven't unpacked everything yet." She paused. "Why did you get out of the car?"

She appreciated him seeing her home, but she had no intentions of asking him inside. Her house was her place. Her own private space. When she had moved to Somerset and found what she thought was the perfect neighborhood along with the perfect house, she had moved in, determined to keep bad memories from past experiences outside. Darius was a reminder of a bad past experience.

"I overheard you mention to Marcy that you had a dripping bathroom faucet that was keeping you awake at night. I thought I'd take care of it for you."

"Now?"

"I don't have anything else I have to do."

Summer sighed. She did. She wanted to take a shower and go to bed. "Thanks for the offer, but I'll get around to calling a plumber later this week."

"No need. It will only take a minute. Then I'll be out of here."

Standing in the shadows, she could barely see the features of his face in the moonlight. But what she did see was a man who had first been her friend and then her lover. She didn't know what he was now, aside from very determined to look out for her.

From the look of things, his mind was made up. She really wanted the faucet fixed. Since he *had* volunteered, she might as well take him up on his offer. "All right, then. Thanks."

"I've told you more than once that you don't ever have to thank me for doing what I do when it involves you, Summer."

She swallowed. Yes, he had said that more than once. Most times had been when they were sitting on a sofa, hugged up while watching television. She'd enjoyed those nights when they would sit curled up with a movie, sharing a bowl of popcorn in her living room, talking.

Another thing she had appreciated about him was that he had never tried pressuring her into sex. That night when they had finally made love, it was because it was something they both wanted, not something he had pushed her into doing.

"Yes, I know you don't need my thanks, but I don't want you to think I don't appreciate it," she finally said.

"Fine. Let me grab my toolbox out the car."

She waited while he went back to his car. Moments

later, she grabbed her mail out of the box and opened the door, hoping she wasn't making a mistake letting him inside.

He followed her and closed the door behind them. The click of the lock made her fully aware that they were alone, totally and completely. Trying to ignore her nerves, she threw the mail on the table. Since she paid most of her bills online, she knew the majority of it was nothing but junk mail anyway.

"Nice place," he complimented, glancing around. She knew he was taking stock of her place.

She tried to ignore how at home he looked in her living room. Like he belonged there. "Thanks."

This house was a lot more spacious than her apartment had been, and since she had a job that paid well, she could afford nice furniture.

"Which bathroom has the dripping faucet?"

"The one in my bedroom." Too late she realized that he was going to go into her most private room.

"Which way?"

"Down the hall to your right."

When he disappeared around the corner, she inhaled deeply, deciding she needed to do something other than just stand there while he repaired the faucet. She needed to at least appear busy. Unfortunately, there weren't any plants she had to water, nor were there dishes in her sink that she needed to wash. Her gaze lit on the junk mail that she had placed on the table and she decided now was as good a time as any to go through it.

* * *

Darius moved down the hall toward Summer's bedroom, thinking she had a lovely home. It was an old house, but very well cared for and maintained. He also liked the vibrant colors that suited her decor and the furnishings that blended in so well. And she was still neat as a pin, he thought, entering her bedroom and glancing around. His gaze came to a stop on the queen-size bed and he couldn't help but wonder what man had probably shared it with her. A rich, older man, no doubt.

Overhearing the conversation about her dripping faucet had given him the perfect excuse to invite himself in. For some reason, he had wanted to see the house that she was living in without him. Although they'd never actually discussed marriage seven years ago, as far as he was concerned, it had been the next thing on the agenda for them. He'd known that after what Whitman had put her through, it would be hard for her to put her trust in any man, but he had been willing to be patient and give her whatever amount of time she needed to learn to trust a man again. She'd needed to know that he was someone she could depend on. Someone who would always be there for her. Too bad she hadn't given them a chance.

Forcing those thoughts from his mind, he headed toward her bathroom. He had just stepped over the threshold and placed the toolbox on the floor when she frantically called out his name.

He rushed to the living room and saw total shock on her face. "Summer? What's wrong?"

She stared up at him, barely able to force words past her lips. But he did hear the one single name she said.

"Tyrone."

He looked at her, confused, not sure why she was bringing up the man who'd caused her nothing but grief. "What about Whitman, Summer?"

She glanced down and he followed her gaze to the mail sprawled at her feet. He quickly figured that something in one of the letters must have upset her.

He bent down, picked up the envelopes and flipped through them. Then he saw a letter from the Texas Parole Board. From the look of the envelope—specifically, all the stamp marks all over it—the post office had made several attempts to deliver it to her.

He pulled out the letter and read it, and then took a deep breath. As a former police officer, he was familiar with Texas law regarding those who'd been victims of violent crimes. A standard letter was issued to notify victims of the parole board's decision to release an inmate.

Darius glanced up at the date of the letter. It had been sent over a month ago. Tyrone Whitman was now a free man.

"I want you to drink this and please don't tell me that you don't need it because you do," Darius said, walking over to where Summer sat on the sofa with a cup of coffee laced with brandy in his hand.

Something had had him on edge all day, and he hadn't been able to figure out what. But now he knew.

The thought that the man who had caused Summer so much grief had only served seven years of a twenty-year sentence made him very angry. But right now, Summer didn't need his anger. More than anything, she needed his support.

Surprisingly, she took the cup without giving him a hard time and took a sip. A frown appeared on her face and he knew why—he had made it a little too strong but if anything, it would help her sleep.

"I can't believe it," she said, breaking the quiet stillness of the room and leaning forward to place the cup on the coffee table. "How can Tyrone be out of prison? That makes no sense."

Darius had to agree with her. It definitely made no sense given the man's crime. They should have put him in jail and thrown away the key. There was no way Whitman should be free to walk around. At least not on this planet. How could they have done such a thing?

He cringed whenever he thought about the final days of the trial and the threats Whitman had shouted out to Summer, saying what he would do to her if he ever got out. He wondered if Summer was remembering those days. He doubted she could forget. She stood and began pacing the floor. He watched her. He of all people knew how she felt, how upset she had to be.

"Tomorrow I'll make a few calls and try to pinpoint his whereabouts," he said, trying to make her feel secure. "Usually when someone who has committed a serious crime is paroled, they're released with a number of restrictions. I bet Whitman can't leave Houston."

She stopped pacing and glanced over at him with blatant hope in her gaze. "You think so?"

"I'll find out tomorrow."

Seeing the panic she was fighting to control gave him pause. At that moment she was no longer the confident, self-assured woman he had watched over the past two weeks. Now there was real fear in her eyes and a sign of helplessness in her voice, and he didn't like it.

Crossing the room he pulled her into his arms. And when she began to tremble while he held her close, whatever hard casting surrounding his heart began to crumble. She needed him and there was no way he could not be there for her.

As if she was relieved to be able to hold on to something solid, she wrapped her arms around him. He was unprepared for the slew of emotions that rushed through him. He would protect her with his life if he had to, and would never let Whitman get close to her again.

He pulled back slightly, wanting to look at her, to make sure she was okay, and when his gaze settled on her lips, he was drawn to them like a magnet. Without any control, he lowered his mouth to hers.

The moment he drew her tongue into his mouth and began feasting on it, he felt sensations all the way to his toes and couldn't do anything but shiver with the pleasure of their intimacy. He drew his arms around her, tightening his hold to bring her body flush with his.

Summer felt his hardness, firm and rigid, pressing

against her and marveled that his body was letting her know how much he wanted her. The only times she'd ever been kissed with such heat and passion was when he did the kissing.

He shifted the angle of his head, which caused her to follow as she tilted the curve of her mouth to his and nearly moaned out loud when his tongue took hold of hers with an intensity that made her weak in the knees.

When he finally released her lips, she leaned into him and sighed deeply. She had needed that kiss. She had needed the connection.

He felt firm, warm and solid—everything she needed at that moment. And in his arms she felt safe and secure. Protected. The thought that Tyrone was no longer locked up behind bars sent real fear through her, fear she was trying hard not to show. But every time she remembered those threats he'd yelled out in the courtroom while being taken away, she couldn't ignore the real panic that wanted to overtake her entire being.

"I don't want you to stay here tonight. You should come home with me, Summer."

She leaned back in his arms and met his gaze. "I can't do that, Darius. I'll be okay and—"

"No, Summer, think about it. I don't want to scare you, but until we know for sure that Whitman is in Houston, I don't want you here alone. What if those two incidents at the shelter had nothing to do with a disgruntled husband or boyfriend? What if Whitman is in violation of his parole and is not in Houston but here in Somerset and responsible for leaving that note on your windshield as well as slashing your tires?"

Darius saw the glint of real fear in her eyes when she considered those possibilities. What he'd said was true. He was not deliberately trying to scare her but she had to face the facts. And until he checked to see just where Whitman was and what he was doing, he would not let her feel safe. Hell, as far as he was concerned, as long as Whitman walked the streets he wouldn't advise Summer to feel safe. She had become an obsession to the man. In Whitman's eyes, she had betrayed him and he intended to teach her a lesson for doing so. He had made that threat in the courtroom with a crazed look in his eyes. Darius would never forget it.

"I'll go back to the shelter and sleep on the sofa in my office, and—"

"And what if word gets around to the women at Helping Hands that you, the woman who counsels them, is in the same predicament they are? Will that offer them any real hope for a brighter future when the man who disrupted your life seven years ago is still doing so?"

Summer's throat tightened as she stared up at him. She wished she could go anywhere but home with him. Being in such close quarters when she was feeling so vulnerable would be temptation she wasn't sure she could handle.

"Go on and pack an overnight bag for now, at least until I find out a few things tomorrow. If I get information indicating Whitman is in Houston behaving himself under the watchful eye of a parole officer, then I'll bring you back here tomorrow. Until then, you're going to be with me, Summer."

Summer breathed in deeply. A part of her wanted to scream out that this had all been a mistake, a nasty nightmare, and she would wake up any minute snuggled in Darius's arms for another reason, one that didn't have anything to do with Tyrone.

Darius released her, dropping his arms. "Get your bag so we can go. I'll wait here."

Summer looked at Darius, knowing his mind was set about her going home with him. There was nothing she could say to make him consider leaving her here tonight. But a part of her didn't want to be here tonight, the part that vividly recalled Tyrone's threats. She was well aware of what the man was capable of.

Because she hadn't lived in town for long, she hadn't gotten to know her neighbors. There were elderly couples that lived on either side of her that she would see on occasion. But other than the staff at the shelter, Darius was the only person she knew in Somerset. She had planned to join some community organizations but hadn't gotten around to doing so.

Making a decision, she said, "All right. It won't take me long to get my things."

A faint smile touched his eyes. "Take your time. I'm not going anywhere."

Her heart felt full. Some things had changed, but Darius was Darius, the man who'd always been and forever would be her knight in shining armor. The one person she could always depend on to be there for her.

Without saying anything else, she rushed off to her bedroom to pack.

# Eight

Summer fell in love with Darius's home the moment she walked through the door. Although it was too dark outside for her to see everything, she knew he had taken her to a sprawling two-story ranch house. When she stepped into his living room, she felt a sense of comfort. She knew it was strange for her to feel that way, but she couldn't help it. During the short drive he had made her feel safe, assuring her that he would find out everything he could about Tyrone's whereabouts and that until he did, she would stay with him.

She glanced around and wondered if he'd hired an interior designer to decorate his home. Everything was color coordinated perfectly, and the furniture complemented the decor. A huge brick fireplace took up one entire wall and a bevy of windows guaranteed sunshine deep in the house during the daylight hours.

To shield the foyer from the interior rooms, a glass-blocked wall was erected between the main living area and the front door. The furniture in the living room was dark, rich leather and looked comfortable as well as sturdy.

"You have a beautiful home, Darius," she said when he followed her inside, carrying her overnight case.

"Thanks. Come on and let me get you settled in the guest room. It's past midnight and you have to be tired."

She was, and couldn't wait to get a good night's sleep, or at least try, she thought. But then she figured that he had to be tired, as well. He had spent the day at both the shelter and the refinery.

Moments later, after following him up a flight of stairs, she stepped into the guest bedroom. She glanced around in total awe. The spacious room had a high roof beam with Old Hickory decor. The king-size bed appeared massive, and the bedspread was a colorful patchwork that matched the country curtains.

"Evidently, your security company is doing well," she said.

When he didn't respond, she glanced over at him and saw a hardness that had formed around his mouth. What had she said to irritate him?

"Darius?"

"Yes, it's doing well," he finally replied in a somewhat biting tone. "There's a guest bath over there with a Jacuzzi tub," he said, pointing across the room. "My bedroom is at the end of the hall if you need anything. Good night."

Summer held her composure as she watched him quickly leave, closing the door behind him. Again she wondered what she had said that had hit a nerve with him. Why had commenting on his success bothered him?

She moved toward the bed and decided that when she saw him in the morning, she would find out.

Darius lay in bed wide awake, staring up at the ceiling. After he'd left Summer, he had made his rounds, making sure everything was locked and secured before going to his bedroom. There he had continued to stew over her comment, which had reminded him that a man's wealth was all she cared about.

He rubbed a hand down his face, not wanting to think that, but what else was he supposed to think? Now that she knew he had a little money, would her attitude toward him change?

He had brought her to his home to protect her, but that didn't mean he had to forgive her for all her past deeds. He wasn't sure that he could. His hands tightened into fists. He heard a sound and glanced over at the illuminated clock on the nightstand. It was almost two in the morning. Since his state-of-the-art security system hadn't sounded to alert him of an intruder, he guessed that Summer was up and moving around in his home. Evidently, she couldn't sleep, either.

Easing out of the bed, he slipped on a pair of jeans. He walked out of his bedroom and immediately saw a light shining downstairs.

When he reached the living room, he didn't see her anywhere. He gently pushed open the kitchen door. She was sitting at the kitchen table drinking what appeared to be a cup of tea, wearing a silk bathrobe belted around the waist. And although he had a feeling she was fighting hard not to do so, he could tell by the trembling of her shoulders that she was crying. Tears from any woman were his downfall—and when they came from Summer, doubly so.

Crossing the room, he fought the tightening of his heart. Hearing his movement, she whipped her head around and met his gaze. But she hadn't been quick enough to wipe away her tears. Without asking what the tears were for, he reached out his arms. "Come here, Summer."

She stared at him for a moment and he wasn't sure exactly what she would do. Then she rose to her feet and crossed the distance separating them. He pulled her into his arms and when he did so, she buried her face in his chest.

"Shh. It's okay, sweetheart. Things are going to be okay."

She shook her head and wiped her eyes, pulling back slightly to look up at him. "No, they're not. I've gotten you upset with me and I don't know why."

At that moment, he felt like a total ass and wished there was a way he could take back his earlier behavior, but he couldn't. So he stood there and held her in his arms, remembering times past when he would hold her the same way just moments before he would claim her mouth with his.

He knew at that moment that his desire for her was just as keen as it had ever been and, unable to fight what he was feeling, he gazed into her face just seconds before using the tip of his tongue to trace a line across her lips.

He heard the catch in her breath and tried to ignore it. He eased closer, unable to stop his body from responding to it. His hard erection pressed against her, warming him in a way he hadn't been warmed in a long time. His tongue left the corners of her mouth to glide over her bottom lip before pulling it into his mouth to suck on it a little. And then there was the feel of her nipples pressing into his bare chest like hardened tips.

He released her bottom lip, but only long enough to press his mouth fully onto hers, needing this taste of her, liking how she trembled in his arms not from fear but from his safekeeping. He had thought about this part of their relationship many times, the moments when he would capture her mouth and take them both to another level. Then one night their kissing had driven them to lose control and they had made love. He continued to kiss her deeply, wanting to lose himself in the kiss again like he had that night. And wanting to lose himself inside of her. He couldn't for the life of him remember connecting to any woman and feeling this way.

"Darius."

The sound of his name sent shudders of arousal through him. It was spoken in a breathless tone, a voice barely able to do anything but purr out a sexy timbre. It made the heat within him rise to a temperature that could easily cause him to boil over.

He shifted his hips and thighs to plaster them closer to the juncture of hers. Every cell within his body felt vibrantly alive, sensitized to her. His mind was finally in sync with what the rest of his body already knew. He wanted her.

He had to have her.

There was no question about his wants and his needs, only about how long he could last without having them satisfied. He pulled back, separating their mouths, but his gaze held hers and he knew she saw in his features the desire he could not hide. His entire being was ruled by an urge to mate with her, to share a physical intimacy to a degree he hadn't had since the last time they'd been together.

While her eyes continued to hold his, she brushed the back of her hand across his cheek and the caress sent shivers through him. He let out the breath he'd been holding, and his hands dropped from her waist to cup her backside, bringing her snug against him.

He could feel the fluttering in her stomach stirring against his erection, making it throb. His nostrils picked up her scent and blood pounded through his veins. He felt himself losing what little control he had and fought to rein it back in. Then she did something he hadn't expected. She made a move he couldn't combat.

She reached out and eased down his zipper before inserting her hands through the opening to cup him, as if she needed to touch, stroke and massage his aroused body part, getting reacquainted with its size and thickness. She didn't break eye contact with him, and he grew even more aroused with her bold ministrations. The more she stroked, the more his body vibrated, making blood rush through his veins, all going directly to that throbbing part of his body.

Minutes ticked by as he continued to stand there and stare at her while she literally drove him over the edge with her hand. He studied her face, saw the intent look in her eyes, the need to touch him this way. There was a feminine glow in her gaze that stirred everything male within him, and then once again, catching him off guard, she leaned in closer, stood on tiptoes and slid her tongue all around his lips, leaving a wet path in its wake. She caressed his mouth with the tip of her tongue the same way her fingertips were now stroking his aroused shaft.

He heard himself groan at the pleasure easing up his spine and he knew if he didn't stop her now, he would embarrass himself in her hands when he preferred being inside of her body.

Now it was his turn to catch her off guard. He gently pushed her hand away seconds before sweeping her into his arms. He leaned down and kissed her with a voraciousness that had her moaning in his mouth.

When he finally pulled away, he took in a deep breath and knew he had to get completely submerged inside her body before he lost it. He stared down at her kiss-swollen lips as he held her in his arms.

"Do you know what you've asked for?" He wanted to make sure they were on the same page.

She held his gaze. "Yes. I know."

"You sure it's what you want?" He had to make doubly sure.

She shifted in his arms and ran her wet, warm tongue across his bare chest. The muscles in his stomach tightened and he knew, without her uttering a single word, he had gotten his answer.

Without saying anything else, he carried her upstairs to his bedroom.

Summer felt hot.

And when Darius placed her on his bed and joined her there, she felt passion that had been bottled up inside of her, ready to boldly claim its freedom. Every bone in her body seemed to vibrate, needing a release.

Her head began spinning when Darius removed her clothes with a swiftness that sent pieces flying everywhere. Then he stood and in record time, dropped his jeans and put on a condom he'd taken out of the nightstand drawer. Moments later, when she lay flat on her back, naked, he towered over her and she felt her thighs quiver with a yearning she hadn't felt in years.

He leaned back to slowly peruse her body and she felt heat every place his eyes touched, especially around her feminine core where his gaze seemed to linger, making sensations stir deep within her. The look in his eyes gave her more than an inkling of what he was thinking, and when he reached out and lifted her hips, placing her legs across his shoulders, she literally cried out before his mouth had a chance to touch her.

She cried out again when his mouth did touch her. He pushed his tongue inside, working it around in her with a greed that sent sparks shooting off in her, scorching everywhere it touched and weakening every bone in her body, turning her muscles to mush.

He spread her legs wider as his mouth continued to inflict upon her torment that was unyielding. What he was doing had captured her senses, totally wrecked her brain cells and fractured all rational thought. Physically, she was beginning to feel herself break into pieces and she grasped the strong arms on each side of her, trying to let him know there was no way she could take any more.

As if determined to prove to her that she could, he continued his torment on her body, tightening his grip on her thighs as his tongue dived deeper inside of her. When he flicked across a sensitive part of her, she shattered, and helplessly screamed his name as an onslaught of sensations ripped into her.

It was only then that he pulled back and straddled her, and before her lungs could fill with more air, he entered her in one deep thrust as he captured one of her breasts into his mouth, sucking deeply on a nipple.

The joining had been so perfect it nearly brought tears to her eyes. She grabbed hold of his head to hold him to her breast and wrapped her legs around him to keep him inside of her. But the movement of his body told her he wasn't going anywhere.

He began moving, retreating and then pushing back in. Over and over again. Harder. Deeper. Faster. She felt every hard inch of him, felt the strong veins of his erection throb deep inside of her and push her over an edge that had her moaning yet again.

And when he shifted his mouth to her other breast and began the same mind-wrecking torment, her moan turned into another scream. She felt every nerve in her body explode, and she began riding a wave that took her across the top of anything and everything. When his body stiffened and bucked mercilessly while he tightly gripped her hips, she knew this was the fusing of not only their bodies, but their minds and souls.

And at that moment, nothing else existed in her world but the man who continued to push in and out of her while screaming her name. This was the same man who'd first shown her how beautiful the joining of a man and woman could be. The same man who moments later slumped down on the bed beside her and pulled her into his arms, holding her as if he never, ever wanted to let her go.

Summer awoke with the sunlight shining on her face and a strong, hard body plastered to her own. She shifted slightly and looked over at the man sleeping beside her, the man whose strong masculine leg was thrown over hers and whose arms, even in sleep, were wrapped around her.

Memories of last night flowed through her mind. It was the first time she had made love in seven years and it had been everything that she had remembered and more. Same man. Same passion. Same love.

She closed her eyes thinking that by rights, she should be upset with herself for still loving him and for the weakness that allowed her to tumble back into bed with him, especially after the way he had cheapened their first night together. But then she couldn't feel remorse when every part of her body was rejuvenated, like it had been awakened from a long sleep by pure pleasure. It had been making love with Darius the last time that had made her appreciate the fact she'd been born a woman, and it was his lovemaking now that was deepening that appreciation.

But still…memories of her pain, her humiliation wouldn't completely go away. How could a man who was so caring when it came to her so easily dishonor her the way he had? She had fallen in love with him completely and when he had made love to her that night, that love had intensified to a point that totally overwhelmed her.

He hadn't said the word *love* to her, but she had been certain of his feelings and had felt he'd displayed with his actions what he hadn't spoken. But she'd discovered her assumptions had been wrong. She did not intend to make the same mistake twice. All she and Darius had just shared was a sexual release. For her, it was a long time coming. She would not assume anything about their relationship ever again. She would accept it for what it was.

He shifted in bed and she tilted her head to look over at him. Before she could say a word, he leaned over and kissed her with a tenderness that made her groan. She didn't have to mull over what they were about to do again, this time in the brightness of the sunlight. And when he eased his body over hers, she wrapped her arms around his neck and eagerly gave him the mouth he seemed so intent to claim.

Summer stood at the window in her office. She kept replaying in her mind what had transpired last night and this morning. Although Darius had made love to her with an intensity and passion that nearly brought tears to her eyes, on the drive back over to her place this morning, she could sense him withdrawing. Why? Was he afraid she might assume just because they had slept together that she would think he wanted her back in his life? If that was the case, then he didn't know how wrong he was about it. She knew better than to think that way. She had learned her lesson well.

He had insisted on driving her to the office after he'd taken her home to dress, and he hadn't had a lot to say about what they had shared last night. Instead, he'd kept the conversation centered on Tyrone and all the things he would be checking on, saying he would take a trip to Houston if he had to.

He was still displaying those protective tendencies,

but she could feel him putting up his guard, shielding emotions from her, keeping them out of her reach. More than once while in his arms last night and this morning, she had been tempted to ask him why he had done what he did seven years ago. But then she would decide to leave well enough alone. What happened was no longer a threat as long as she kept her heart out of the mix. Besides, she had bigger fish to fry. Tyrone Whitman and his whereabouts were what she needed to stay focused on. It was the only thing she should care about, the only thing that mattered.

The thought of Tyrone being free made her skin crawl, but she refused to allow him to make her live in total fear. More than ever she was convinced he was the one who'd left that note on her windshield and slashed her tires, mainly because those were things Tyrone would do. Saying he took care of his own was something he'd said to her more than once. The reason she hadn't made the connection before was because she had assumed he was still locked up in prison. But now she knew that was not the case.

She glanced up at the clock on the wall. Darius said he would be coming back to walk her over to the café for lunch, and not to leave without him. This would be one time she did what he asked without any hesitation.

The phone on her desk rang and she immediately went to pick it up, hoping it was Darius with good news. "Hello?"

The person on the other end didn't say anything. "Hello?" she repeated. Chills ran down her spine when the person finally hung up. She tried to convince herself it was probably just a misdialed number. But deep down she had a feeling that wasn't true.

Darius's hands tightened on the steering wheel as he turned down the street that would take him to Helping Hands. Already he was regretting the news he was about to deliver to Summer.

He had made a call to the Houston Police Department as soon as he'd dropped Summer off at work. He'd been told Walt was out of town on an investigation, so he had spoken with Manny, another detective he knew. It had taken Manny less than an hour to find out what he wanted to know.

Manny had verified Whitman was out on parole with an order not to leave Houston. However, according to Manny, Whitman could not be found at what should have been his current address, and his landlord hadn't seen him in weeks. Since Whitman had a week or so left before they could haul him in for violating parole, so far he hadn't broken any laws…unless it could be proven he had left Houston.

There was no doubt in Darius's mind that Whitman had been in Somerset and was possibly still around. Since Somerset was such a small town, it would be easy for Whitman to find out where Summer worked—as well as where she lived. The thought of her being at Whitman's mercy again was enough to make every fiber of his being roar in anger.

He shifted his thoughts to last night and this morning.

While making love to her, he had tried holding himself back but he hadn't been able to control his emotions. Never had he been so affected by making love to a woman. It was as if the last seven years hadn't existed and there had never been a wedge between them. Last night and this morning fit perfectly into his plans. After this morning, he was supposed to take her back home, tell her about all the wealth he had accumulated over the years, that he was a member of the TCC and that not only did he know Kevin Novak but that Kevin was one of his closest friends. He had wanted to see the hurt in her eyes.

But Whitman's parole made that impossible—at least that's what he told himself. If it was determined the man was a threat to Summer, that would mean she'd stay with him for a while. She wouldn't like the idea, but he was determined to protect her at all costs.

Summer had been hoping, praying that the last seven years in jail would have changed Tyrone and she would no longer matter to him. It was disheartening to know she had been wrong and there was a strong chance he was stalking her again.

She told Darius about the strange phone call she had gotten that morning, and he, too, was convinced it had been Tyrone.

"Come on, let's go to lunch."

During lunch at the café Darius received a call. After the conversation ended, Summer knew from the look on his face that she was not going to like what he had to say.

He proved her right. "Before coming to the shelter I stopped at police headquarters to alert them that Whitman might be in the area. I provided them with a description of how he looked the last time I saw him, figuring his looks hadn't changed much over the years. But even if they had, Somerset is a small enough town that a stranger would stick out like a sore thumb."

He stopped talking, but she could tell there was more. "And?" she prompted.

"And they think he's been seen. A couple of the police officers who were cruising the area a few blocks from the shelter got suspicious of a guy who met Whitman's description. When they tried to approach him to question him, he ran."

Summer didn't say anything for a moment. "I refuse to let Tyrone scare me again, Darius. Although it didn't work the last time, I'm going to get another restraining order."

"That's a good idea. If he is taken into custody here in Somerset for any reason, his parole will automatically be revoked."

Darius hesitated a moment and then said, "Although you're refusing to let Tyrone scare you, I'm hoping you'll continue to stay with me until this issue with him is resolved. It will only be a matter of time before he finds out where you live, if he doesn't know already. Alarm or no alarm, if he ever breaks inside your home again, depending on his frame of mind, there's no telling what he will do. If knowing he will go back to jail and serve out the rest of his sentence hasn't deterred him, that can only mean he doesn't care. And people who don't care will do just about anything to get back at the person they think has betrayed them."

Summer knew what Darius said was true. Tyrone had held a gun to her head, willing and ready to end her life as well as his own. She really didn't want to go home with Darius again, but she didn't have a choice. Even after what they had shared last night and this morning, she could still feel tension between them. She could tell he still had his guard up.

"Summer?"

She met his gaze, felt the heat in the dark depths of his eyes. He wanted to keep her safe. And he wanted her. Summer knew that no matter how guarded he was being, he couldn't deny he enjoyed having her back in his bed, and she would admit she enjoyed being there. Intimacy between them wasn't just good, it was off the charts. Sexual tension was always oozing between them, even when she didn't want it to, like now.

Knowing he was waiting on an answer, she said, "Okay, I'll move in with you for the time being if you think it will be for the best."

# Nine

A week later, as Darius sat in the TCC café waiting to meet with Lance, he was convinced that Summer moving in with him had been the best thing to keep her safe. Although he wasn't sure just what her being underfoot was doing to his peace of mind.

At first, he had put up his guard, finding excuses to work outdoors in the evenings to stay away from the house. But living under the same roof made it difficult to deny his desire for her when she was near.

Evidently, she hadn't been sure just where she should sleep the night she had returned to his place. They had stopped by her house to get more of her things, and after she had gotten settled at his place and taken a shower, she had gone to sleep in the guest bedroom.

He had stayed outside deliberately talking to his ranch foreman, and when he had come inside and found her asleep in the guest bedroom, he tried to convince himself that her sleeping arrangements were fine with him.

He'd taken a shower and crawled into his own bed. But knowing that she was asleep in another bedroom didn't suit him. However, his stubbornness, the cold hard casting around his heart, just wouldn't thaw any.

After the third night, he realized that he had finally reached his limit. He got out of bed and went into the guest bedroom to discover her wide awake. She had been unable to sleep those nights, too.

He could vividly recall that particular night, and how he had stood in the doorway and stared at her across the room, wanting so much to despise her, and also his weakness for her. Without saying a word, he had reached out his hand to her and she had eased out of bed, crossing the room to place her hand in his.

Darius sighed deeply thinking it had been at that particular moment that he could no longer deny that she was and would always be a part of him. He had faced the truth that the reason he was so determined to protect her was because he still cared for her. Deeply.

Since then she had shared his bed every night and he'd enjoyed waking up with her beside him each morning. And he was getting used to her being in his home, in his space. Being under the same roof with her gave him a chance to get to know the new Summer, the one that had grown up without him. And he couldn't help but admire the woman she had become, the dedicated social worker who understood what it was like to be a woman in jeopardy. A woman who had been abused.

In the evenings he no longer found reasons to stay away from his home. Together they would prepare meals, clean up the kitchen and talk about the day's events, only bringing up Whitman when they needed to. He had been sighted several more times in Somerset. Darius had even approached the Texas Rangers about Whitman informing them that he had violated parole. Although he had yet to be apprehended, Darius was convinced that eventually he would be, and was glad, in the meantime, that he was keeping Summer safe.

"Sorry I'm late. I sort of got detained," Lance said, breaking into his thoughts and sliding into the chair across from him.

Darius couldn't help but laugh. Based on the satisfied smile on his best friend's face, he could only assume Kate was the reason he was late, and now he understood what it was like to have a woman under your skin and close at hand.

"No problem. I just wanted to give you a copy of the official fire department report and provide an update on my investigation. I checked out all your employees who were questionable and was able to rule out each and every one of them."

Lance nodded. "I figured you would. I told you who I suspect."

Yes, Lance had told him, Darius thought, several times. But Darius still wasn't convinced. Something didn't sit right with him.

Darius checked his watch. It had become a routine for him to drive Summer to work every morning and pick her up in the afternoon, and he did not want to be late. It was a routine he was beginning to get accustomed to. And it was one he liked, whether he wanted to admit it or not. Business would have to wait.

Summer came down the stairs and looked around, not seeing Darius anywhere. She went into the kitchen, deciding to make a cup of tea. It wasn't unusual for him to go outside and spend time with the men who ran his ranch in the afternoons, and she had been fully aware that when she'd first come to stay with him he had used that as an excuse to put distance between them.

Now that had changed. He no longer avoided her in his home and she spent every night in his bed. She still wasn't assuming anything and knew once Tyrone had been captured, Darius would expect her to leave and return to her home. She wouldn't be doing herself any favors if she became attached to his beautiful home, which she already loved. It was far enough from town to offer peace and quiet that anyone would cherish, yet at the same time it was a place where a family could be raised.

She shook her head, determined to get such foolish thoughts out of it. What she and Darius were sharing was physical and nothing more. She turned at the sound of footsteps and knew it was him.

He walked through the back door, saw her and smiled. He might not love her but there was no doubt in her mind that he enjoyed having her around. He closed the door behind him, locked it and just stood there, staring at her. When he had brought her home from work she had gone upstairs to take a shower. Now she felt refreshed but at the same time, hot. And the way he was looking at her was making her feel even hotter.

Without a word, she crossed the kitchen floor and wrapped her arms around his neck. Then, leaning upward she captured his mouth with hers. His response was immediate and he didn't waste any time letting her know it, or letting her feel it. His thick erection was throbbing against her, making her senses come unglued and sending sensations rushing through her veins and all over her skin.

Moments later she pulled back and met his gaze. "We need to prepare dinner," she said in a ragged voice, barely able to breathe.

"Later." And then he swept her off her feet and headed upstairs to his bedroom.

Bodies joined. Summer moved with Darius as his lips brushed a kiss beneath her ear and whispered just how much he enjoyed being inside of her, making love to her, being one with her.

The rhythm he had established was perfect, and floated them toward fulfillment. The air surrounding them was charged and the more he thrust into her body, the more her senses seemed whipped with a pleasure so profound it took her breath away.

"Now!"

As if on cue, her body began convulsing right along with his, endlessly, as shivers tore through them, pulling them down yet at the same time building them up. And when she cried out in pleasure, every pull of her feminine muscles was regulated by his steady yet rapid strokes into her body, making her lift her hips and use her thighs to squeeze him tight, clench him for all she was worth.

She tossed her head back when he surged even deeper inside of her, gripping her thighs and taking her all over again, pushing her toward another orgasm and doing everything in his power to make sure they both got there.

They did.

Instead of letting up, the heat was on yet again, and the workings of her inner muscles signified that such a notion made perfect sense, given the depth of their desire, their passion and their sexual hunger. It was as if they were making up for lost time and then some, filling a drought, satisfying a yearning, soothing an ache.

And when he began moving inside of her in quick, rapid successions, she cried out his name as shivers of pleasure tore through her once again.

"Do you know how beautiful you are? And you're even more beautiful after making love."

Summer glanced over and saw Darius had awakened. He was smiling, and the look in his eyes was filled with the same heat she still felt on some parts of her body. "Thank you."

She knew at that moment she would have to broach the subject she had tried putting behind her since seeing him again.

His betrayal.

"And you are a very handsome man, making love or not," she said softly. Truthfully. She paused a moment and then asked the one question she needed answered. One she could not put off asking any longer. "Why did you make that bet?"

A confused look appeared on his face. "What bet?"

Summer was certain there was no way he could not know what bet she was referring to. But if he wanted to pretend to have a loss of memory, she could remedy that. "I'm talking about the bet you made with Walt about how quick you could take me to bed."

In an instant, he was up, leaning over her. The look on his face was one of incredulous fury. "What the hell are you talking about? I never made a bet like that."

She wondered why he was not going to own up to it now. "That's all right, Darius. It doesn't matter."

"Yes, it does matter," he said in a hard voice. "Especially if you believed it."

She frowned. "Why are you denying it?"

"Because I never did such a thing. How could you have believed something like that?"

She drew in a deep breath and held his gaze. "Because Walt told me what you did. He felt that I had a right to know."

His face hardened. “Walt!” he all but roared.

“Yes,” she countered in a voice filled with just as much conviction. “Yes, Walt Stewart. He was your partner at the time. Or have you forgotten about him, as well?”

“No, I haven’t forgotten about Walt. In fact, I spoke with him just last week about that arson case I’m investigating. What you’re saying doesn’t make sense, Summer, because Walt knew how I felt about you. There’s no way he could have told you something like that.”

Summer’s head began spinning and it took her a second to find steady ground. *Walt knew how I felt about you…*

Could he be saying that he had cared as deeply about her as she had about him? She continued to stare at Darius and noted the way he was looking back at her. Then he asked slowly, with disbelief, “And Walt actually told you that?”

“Yes.”

Darius released her and eased out of bed, seemingly barely able to keep the lid on raging anger. She swallowed, slowly realizing the impact of what now appeared to be a blatant lie. But why?

“Put on some clothes. We need to talk, and this is not the place for us to do it,” he said, interrupting her thoughts. He picked up his jeans and eased into them. “Please meet me in the living room.”

Summer stared at his back as he walked out the room.

* * *

Darius paced his living room with his hands in tight fists. Why in the hell had Walt told Summer something like that? How could he have told her?

He could vividly remember sharing a beer with Walt one night after their shift had ended and telling him just how much Summer had come to mean to him. Walt had sat there listening, not saying anything, mainly because Darius hadn't given him a chance to say anything. His heart had been filled with love, and he had wanted to share those emotions with someone he had considered a friend.

He and Walt had gotten hired around the same time and had easily become friends. He was well aware of Walt's issues with the opposite sex because of his ex-wife's betrayal, but Darius had overlooked them because it hadn't been his issue or concern.

Now he had to wonder just how deep Walt's deception went. He knew what Summer had been told, but what about what Walt had told him about Summer, and the message she had supposedly left for him? According to Walt, Summer had left town with an older man. A rich man.

"I'm here now."

Darius stopped his pacing and turned around. She stood there, not in the shorts and blouse he had taken off her earlier that night, but in one of his T-shirts that had been thrown across a chair in his room. Whether it was her intent or not, her wearing his shirt meant something to him. It was as if she was giving him an unspoken acknowledgment of their connection, a connection that had started seven years ago and by some work of miracle was back in full force.

Making love to her over the past weeks had closed old wounds. But now he was discovering that those wounds were self-inflicted due to his belief of Walt's lies. "Let's sit and discuss this, please. I'm beginning to think we've been played."

He watched as she took a seat on the sofa, trying not to notice that his shirt hit her mid-thigh, and how sexy she looked in it. More than anything, he had to keep his mind on the issues at hand, issues they needed to dissect and resolve. After she was seated, instead of sitting beside her on the sofa, he took the leather wing chair that sat not far away.

"To take up the conversation we started in bed, I want you to know, I want you to believe, that at no time did I discuss sleeping with you with Walt. There was no bet."

He watched her features. She held his gaze as intensely as he was holding hers. He saw in her eyes a desire to believe what he said. But…

"Then how did he know about that night?" she asked. "He knew that you had spent the night over at my place."

Darius thought about her words. "He must have driven by your apartment and seen my car parked out front."

He could tell from her expression that she was taking his explanation into consideration, agreeing that it was possible. However, there was still lingering doubt in her eyes.

"Why didn't you contact me?" she then asked him. "He told me you left town and would be gone for a few days, but I never heard from you again. It was like you *had* scored and put me out of your life."

Darius leaned back in his chair. "Did he not tell you why I had to leave immediately or where I had gone?"

"He didn't go into any details. He just said you'd been called away on police business and would be gone a few days."

Darius jaw tightened. "The reason I had to leave when I did was because I got a call that Ethan had been critically injured in a car accident and was being wheeled into surgery. Since I'm his only family, I had to get to Charleston. For a while, I wasn't sure Ethan was going to make it. I was by his bedside day and night and did not have use of my cell phone. And when I did call, I got a message that you had gotten your cell number changed."

He saw the shock in Summer's gaze and before she could say anything, he knew she hadn't known. "Walt didn't tell me that," she said angrily, getting to her feet. "I didn't know."

Connecting his fingers in a steeple, he placed them under his chin. "When I returned to town almost two weeks later, after Ethan's condition had stabilized, I went straight to your place from the airport, only to be told by your landlord that you had moved out a few days earlier, and that an older man in a Mercedes had picked you up and that you had left with him."

She nodded. "Yes, that was Karl Lindsey."

He paused for a second and then said, "Walt is the one who told me why you had left."

She shifted in her seat and his gaze was drawn to a flash of her thigh. His attention went back to her face when she said, "Yes, Walt just happened to drop by that day Karl was there, and just on the off chance you cared enough to ask, I told him that I had taken a job with Karl and would be moving to Florida for a year."

Darius raised a brow. "A job?"

"Yes, Karl had been one of my regulars at the restaurant. He's a writer. He offered me a job as his assistant, editing and organizing his notes. He had offered me the same job before but Tyrone had forced me to turn it down. When I hadn't heard anything from you, and after Walt told me what you did, I decided to take Mr. Lindsey's offer and moved to Florida with him and his wife and—"

"His wife?"

Summer didn't say anything for a moment as she studied his expression. Then she said, "Yes, Lola, his wife. You sound surprised."

Darius stared at her as a deep sharp pain ripped through him. For the first time he was seeing that trust on both sides had been shattered because he and Summer had been quick to believe the lies of others. He had been so quick to believe the worst of her and she of him. Not because they thought of each other as devious people, but because their relationship had been in the early stages, at a very delicate period when trust, faith and love was building. He didn't want to think of how strong their relationship would be if it had been given a chance to grow.

"Darius?"

He hated telling her what he'd thought, what he'd assumed, but knew that he had to do so. "The message Walt gave me, the one he claimed you left, was that you had met this old, rich man and that you couldn't waste your time with someone who was nothing but a college-educated cop with no aspirations of being anything else."

She stared at him. He saw the hurt and pain in her eyes and knew why. Just like she had believed Walt's lies about him, he had believed the man's lies about her.

"Why were we so quick to believe the worst of each other?" she asked in a whisper that he could barely hear. "We played right into Walt's hands," she added. "That's sad."

As far as he was concerned, it was worse than sad. It was pathetic. Seven years wasted. He then said the only thing that he could say at that moment. "I'm sorry."

She breathed in deeply. "And I'm sorry, as well."

Darius could only sit there silently for a moment, wondering how one went about repairing a love that had been destroyed by lies. Lies that had been so easy to accept. Inside of him, a voice said, *One day at a time.*

"Summer, I—"

"No, Darius, I think we both need time to come to terms with what happened, the lies that were told and why we were so quick to believe them. I haven't been in a relationship with anyone since you, serious or otherwise. I've grown accustomed to being by myself, not wanting a man to share my life. I don't trust easily anymore. I'm more cautious. I really don't know if that can change."

He could read between the lines. She was letting him know when it was all said and done, regardless of the fact that they had lived together for the last few weeks or so, getting along marvelously, complementing each other's personalities, she was not all that certain that she wanted to give them another chance because of their lack of faith and trust in each other. From what she was saying, she still didn't want a man in her life. Things had changed. She had changed. In a way, he understood.

Over the years he had kept most women at bay, being selective about who he wanted to spend his time with and not allowing himself to get serious about anyone. But he could see all that changing and wondered if she could. Their relationship—and he considered them to be in a relationship—had to undergo some serious repairs. Major repairs. But he thought they could do it.

They had uncovered a lot tonight. But he still had something else to come clean about—his association with the TCC.

"Summer. I—"

"Will you contact the authorities to see if anyone has seen Tyrone again?" she cut in to ask.

He knew she was trying to get off the subject. He would let her do so for now since tonight had been overwhelming, to say the least, and he wasn't sure how she would handle the unveiling of another lie. One that had been his own, as a way to hurt her. He would tell her another time. Soon. Tomorrow.

"Yes, I'll do that."

There was no need to tell her that he planned on killing two birds with one stone by driving to Houston tomorrow to meet with Tyrone's parole officer and that he would also be paying a visit to Walt.

He studied her, wondering if she knew the significance of what she had admitted moments ago. He was the last man she had made love with. She hadn't wanted a man in her life in seven years, yet she had shared herself with him.

At that moment, all he could think about was what they had shared. The heat. The passion.

"I guess we could sit here and stare at each other all night," she finally said, "but I prefer going back to bed."

He rose to his feet, accepting the gravity of the mistakes they'd both made. But he also accepted that she needed him now like he needed her. "Then I don't plan to keep you up any longer."

He crossed the room to her. They had a lot left to talk about, still more truths to tell. But at that moment, they needed to be together and they both knew it.

Darius held his hand out to her and she took it. Together, they returned to his bedroom.

* * *

While en route to the shelter the next morning, Darius received a call. "This is Darius."

He listened attentively to what the caller was saying and then he said, "That's good news and I appreciate you calling to let me know. I'll pass the information on to Ms. Martindale."

He clicked off the phone and glanced over at Summer. "That was a Texas Ranger friend of mine. He was calling to let me know that they picked up Whitman this morning."

Darius saw a wave of relief pass through her. "Where?" she asked.

They had come to a stop at the traffic light and Darius glanced over at her. "Less than a block from your house."

He hated telling her the next part but knew that he had to. "He had a gun and a rope in his possession."

Summer stiffened and Darius understood why. Chances were Whitman had discovered where she lived, and a good possibility existed that he had planned on using that information for no good. Since he had violated parole in more ways than one, Darius knew he would return to prison and serve his entire sentence.

She didn't say anything, staring straight ahead, out the windshield.

"You okay?" he asked.

She turned to him. "Yes, I'm okay."

She might be okay, but he wasn't. How could he

have been so wrong about her? He couldn't wait to confront Walt about the lies he'd told. "I have something to take care of this morning and won't be back in time to join you for lunch."

"All right."

She didn't seem to be in a talkative mood and he figured she needed time to digest everything he had told her about Whitman.

"Since Tyrone is in police custody, there's no reason I can't return home now, is there?"

*None other than I don't want you to go. I've gotten used to having you around. I've fallen in love with you all over again.* "No, there's no reason you can't," he said.

He breathed in deeply and at that moment, he knew there was no use denying what he'd known all along. He loved her. He had not stopped loving her.

And all this time he had tried convincing himself that he would seek revenge for what she had done, when he knew he couldn't have gone through with that plan no matter how much he'd thought he wanted to hurt her.

From the first moment she had turned her eyes on him he had been a goner, and although he'd convinced himself over the years that he had gotten over her, the simple truth was, he hadn't. Coming to terms with his love for her was a monumental release of the hold he'd placed on his emotions. All the built-up tension and anger he'd felt since seeing her again left his body, flowed out of his muscles. It strengthened his heart, propelling him to do whatever he had to do to make her his again.

# Ten

A few hours later, Summer slipped into her walking shoes to go to the café for lunch, reflecting that this was the first time in quite a while that she would be doing so without Darius by her side.

She drew in a huge breath of profound relief, knowing what could have been another nightmare with Tyrone was now over. She shivered when she thought of the items that had been in his possession. There was no doubt in her mind he intended to do her harm, and she was grateful yet again to Darius for keeping her out of harm's way.

Darius. The man she still loved.

She wondered if she'd sounded convincing when she told him that she didn't want a man in her life. A part of her did want to belong to him, totally and completely, but was afraid to get her hopes up again. Even though she knew the truth now, it couldn't erase the pain she had felt for seven years.

Besides, there was nothing Darius had said to make her think that he wanted to renew what they'd once shared. When she'd mentioned returning to her place now that the threat with Tyrone was over, he hadn't said anything to talk her out of it, he hadn't said that he didn't want her to leave.

He had apologized for believing the lies Walt had told him. And she had apologized to him, as well. Later, they had made love but no promises had been made. There had been no discussion of a future together. Although he hadn't said as much, she had a feeling that he didn't want a woman in his life.

That left her with the same life she'd been living since leaving Houston. The kind of life she had gotten used to. It was somewhat lonely but safe. She would continue to live it without the man she loved.

The anger within Darius told him to strike out the moment he saw Walt walking toward him. But he fought to hold his rage in check. There was only one thing he wanted from the man and that was for him to explain why he'd done what he did.

Without telling Walt why, he had called and requested to meet with him in Laverne Square, a newly developed area of Houston near the Madaris Office

Park. He rose from the bench when he saw the curious look in Walt's eyes.

"Darius, didn't you get my message that the guy you wanted me to check out was clean? I left it on your voice mail last week."

"That's not why I asked you to meet with me," Darius answered, trying to keep the bitterness out of his voice.

Walt lifted a brow. "Oh. Then what's up?"

Darius looked directly into his eyes. "I'm here about the lie you told me about Summer Martindale."

Walt held his gaze for an instant before shifting his eyes to look out over the pond in the square. Time stretched on and for a moment, Darius wondered if he was going to say anything. Then Walt turned his gaze to Darius.

"She came with a lot of baggage and was trouble with that crazy boyfriend of hers. You didn't need her."

His words, spoken as if he'd had a right to make that decision, slithered down Darius's spine. "You were wrong, Walt. She wasn't trouble and you knew how I felt about her. I not only needed her but I loved her."

"You have a lot to learn about women, Darius. You can never let one get under your skin, and you can never admit to loving one."

Darius stared at him for a moment. "Actually," he said in a deep, cutting tone, "there's a lot that *you* need to learn about them, and recognizing a good one when you meet her is at the top of the list."

A deep frown settled on Walt's face. "There aren't any good ones."

Walt had extreme issues, but Darius couldn't concern himself with that right now. As far as he was concerned, what Walt had done was unforgivable. When he thought about all those wasted years when he and Summer could have been together, years when he had loathed her very name, he practically wanted to kill the man. It was all for nothing. All for lies.

Filled with total disgust and having nothing else to say, Darius started to leave.

"Hey, wait, man, we're okay, aren't we? We're still friends?" Walt asked in a lighthearted tone.

Darius stopped walking and looked over his shoulder. Their gazes locked. The message he was certain Walt saw in his eyes was blatantly clear.

"No. Our friendship died the day you lied to me. I loved her, but because I thought you were my friend, I believed you. A true friend would not have done what you did."

Without saying anything else, he walked off, leaving Walt standing there.

Summer was just about to go to the café when one of the security guards escorted a very well dressed, distinguished-looking older man through the entrance. It didn't take a rocket scientist to figure out from the way the man was carrying himself that he was someone of authority, someone of importance, which could only mean he was a member of the TCC. Kevin Novak had given her a heads-up that over the next few months, members of the TCC would probably be dropping by to check out the shelter since he had asked them for more money.

Putting on her brightest smile, Summer crossed the lobby to greet the man. "Welcome to Helping Hands," she said, extending her hand to him. "I'm Summer Martindale, a social worker here."

The man took her hand and looked at her. "So, you're the young woman who's been causing so much excitement."

Summer forced her smile to remain intact when she recognized his voice. He was the person she had talked to on the phone when she'd called requesting additional security guards. "Am I?" she couldn't help but ask, not liking the way the man seemed to be staring down his nose at her.

"Yes. I'm Sebastian Huntington, a member of the Texas Cattleman's Club."

"Nice to meet you, Mr. Huntington."

He didn't say anything to indicate that the feelings were mutual. Instead, he glanced around. "Things seem calm enough around here. I really don't see why two guards are needed. But then, you've managed to convince Kevin Novak differently."

She was about to say the reason things appeared calm was because everyone felt safer with two guards when he once again looked down his nose at her and arrogantly said, "And then there's Darius Franklin, who's evidently quite taken with you. He's also been singing your praises at the TCC meetings." A sneer touched his lips as he studied her features. "Now I see why."

Surprise flickered in her eyes. "Darius?"

"Yes. He's one of our newest members."

Now she was confused. *Darius was a member of TCC?*

"How long has he been a member?"

The man frowned down at her like she'd asked a stupid question. "Not long enough for him and his friends to be throwing their weight around. He's only been a member for over a year."

Summer nodded. "Oh, I see." And the sad part of it was that she really did see. Darius had lied to her.

"Ready to go?"

Summer slowly lifted her gaze from the document at the sound of the deep, husky voice. Had it been nearly three weeks ago when here in this office she had heard that voice again for the first time in seven years?

After Mr. Huntington left, instead of walking to the café, she had gone to the library. There she had researched information on the Texas Cattleman's Club branch that was located in Somerset. Darius was listed as a member, having joined the same day as Kevin Novak and several other men, and from the photographs she had seen, it was apparent that he and Mr. Novak knew each other very well. Why had he pretended otherwise when she'd told him of her meeting with Mr. Novak? Why had he deliberately kept his membership in the TCC from her?

Instead of answering his question, she asked one of her own.

"Why didn't you tell me you were a member of the Texas Cattleman's Club?"

She saw surprise light his eyes and knew he was probably wondering how she'd found out. "Mr. Huntington dropped by to check out the place and mentioned you're a member," she said, leaning back in her chair.

"So, my question is, why didn't you tell me, Darius? You had several chances to do so when I was preparing for my meeting with Mr. Novak, and many after that. Why didn't you tell me?"

A part of Darius wished he'd have told Summer everything last night. How would she react to finding out he had withheld the information because of his plan to hurt her?

Any chance of rebuilding a relationship with her would probably be destroyed now. But still, he had to be upfront and honest with her. Lies were the reason they were in the situation they were in now.

Sighing deeply, he entered her office and closed the door behind him, leaning against it. "The reason I didn't want to tell you is because I was still operating under the belief that you had left Houston with a rich man. A man you had chosen over me because of his wealth. With that belief festering in my mind as well as my heart over the years, I had grown to resent you for choosing wealth over love."

When she didn't say anything, he continued. "I figured that if that was true, once you found out about my wealth, the fact that I had become successful, I could get my revenge by seducing you, taking you to bed and then walking away from you the same way I thought you had walked away from me. I wanted to hurt you the way you had hurt me."

Summer still didn't say anything for a moment, and then in a low voice, she asked, "You hated me that much?"

Darius breathed in again, hearing the deep hurt in her voice. "I thought I did, but once I got to know what I thought was the new Summer Martindale, the one who's dedicated to the women at the shelter, the one who works tirelessly after hours when her shift is over, I realized that no matter how much I wanted revenge, I couldn't have gone through with it. And do you know why, Summer?"

"I have no idea," she said in a sharp tone.

He held her gaze. "Because I realized that although I'd tried over the years, I couldn't replace love with hate. Although I wanted to hurt you, I couldn't because I still love you."

Their gazes held and for a moment, he wondered if she believed him. He hoped and prayed for some sort of sign that she did. He had been wrong for wanting to get even with her, but at the time he'd felt it was something he had needed to do because of his pain.

"So many years have passed, Summer. We owe it to ourselves to try and rebuild the relationship that was destroyed because of our lack of faith and trust in each other. In Houston today, I made a point to see

Walt. I had to know why he'd done what he did. His reason was he saw me falling for you and figured I'd get hurt. But the truth of the matter is that I was hurt in the end anyway. Not by you, but because I'd believed the worst about you."

He moved away from the door to stand in front of her desk. "I'm asking that you give me a chance to do what I wanted to do seven years ago and that is, love you the way a man is supposed to love a woman. Please allow me into your heart, Summer. Give me a chance to prove that I am the right man for you."

He took another step closer. "Will you put behind you all the hurt and lies of before and move forward in the way we should have years ago? Can you find it in your heart to love me as much as I love you? To work on rebuilding a relationship of love, trust and faith?"

He saw the single tear that fell from her eye and literally held his breath before she began speaking.

"Yes," she said slowly. "I can work on rebuilding our relationship because I love you, too, and I want you in my life. I want a future with you, not because of your wealth but because you are a man who's proven more than once that he can be there when I need someone, that he has my best interests at heart, and protects me when I need protecting."

She pushed her chair back and walked around her desk to him. "We have a lot of years to make up for, but I knew that night we made love again it was something I wanted. I was just afraid to hope for it."

Darius pulled her into his arms and held her tight, close to his heart. And then he lowered his mouth to hers. He wanted her with him always and from the intensity of their kiss, it seemed she wanted the very same thing.

Moments later, he pulled his mouth away from hers. "Ready to go home, sweetheart?" And to make sure she understood, he added, "Not to your place, but to mine. A place that you will one day consider ours, I hope."

She smiled up at him. "Yes, I'm ready."

He took her hand in his and they walked out of her office together. He knew there was a lot of work ahead, rebuilding their relationship into the kind they both wanted, the kind they deserved. Lies had destroyed their relationship, but love had restored it. Their love would make it all happen for them.

They would make sure of it. Together.

# Epilogue

*Three weeks later*

Summer stepped outside on the porch and glanced around. It was a beautiful day and the smell of flowers was everywhere.

She felt butterflies move around in her stomach at the same time she saw the car pull into the yard. She smiled. Darius was home.

She glanced around again, thinking how easy it was to think of his ranch as home. She never returned to her place, and every week more and more of her things would show up here.

And then one night while they were busy unpacking some more of her boxes, he had got down on his knee and proposed to her. He asked her to be his wife, the mother of his babies and his best friend for life. Somehow through her tears she had accepted. The moment he had slipped the ring on her finger, more love and happiness than she'd ever thought possible filled her heart. They hadn't set a date yet, and had decided to take things one day at a time.

She had met his friends and could see the special friendship they shared. She liked them a lot. Tonight they would be joining Lance and Kate at the TCC for dinner.

As soon as the car came to a stop, she moved down the steps, and when Darius opened the door and got out, she was there waiting.

He pulled her into his arms and kissed her, making her feel wanted and loved. Things were so good between them that she would occasionally pinch herself to make sure it was real. And over and over he would prove to her that it was.

He pulled back and studied her face with concern. "Are you okay? I stopped by the shelter and Marcy said you had left early."

She smiled up at him. "Yes, I'm fine. I just wanted to be here when you got home. I thought that I would pamper you a little before we left for dinner."

A grin curved his lips and she could tell he liked the idea. "Pamper me?"

"Yes. Are you interested?"

Instead of answering, he swept her off her feet into his arms and carried her up the steps. *Yes,* she thought, *he was interested.*

She laughed, knowing once he got her inside the house he intended to show her just how interested he was.

* * * * *

*Don't miss the next story in the*
TEXAS CATTLEMAN'S CLUB *collection,*
*TEXAN'S WEDDING-NIGHT WAGER,*
*available next month from*
*Silhouette Desire.*

RICK'S APPOINTMENT with his attorney early Wednesday morning went only moderately better than his meeting with social services the day before. The prognosis wasn't great—but at least his attorney was going to file a motion for DNA testing. Just so Rick could petition to see the child…his sister's baby. The sister he didn't know he had until it was too late.

The rest of what his attorney said had been downhill from there.

Cell phone in hand before he'd even reached his Nitro, Rick punched in the speed dial number he'd programmed the day before.

Maybe foster parent Sue Bookman hadn't received his message. Or had lost his number. Maybe she didn't want to talk to him. At this point he didn't much care what she wanted.

"Hello?" She answered before the first ring was complete. And sounded breathless.

Young and breathless.

"Ms. Bookman?"

"Yes. This is Rick Kraynick, right?"

"Yes, ma'am."

"I recognized your number on caller ID," she said, her voice uneven, as though she was still engaged in whatever physical activity had her so breathless to begin with. "I'm sorry I didn't get back to you. I've been a little…distracted."

The words came in more disjointed spurts. Was she jogging?

"No problem," he said, when, in fact, he'd spent the better part of the night before watching his phone. And fretting. "Did I get you at a bad time?"

"No worse than usual," she said, adding, "Better than some. So, how can I help?"

God, if only this could be so easy. He'd ask. She'd help. And life could go well. At least for one little person in his family.

It would be a first.

"Mr. Kraynick?"

"Yes. Sorry. I was… Are you sure there isn't a better time to call?"

"I'm bouncing a baby, Mr. Kraynick. It's what I do."

"Is it Carrie?" he asked quickly, his pulse racing.

"How do you know Carrie?" She sounded defensive, which wouldn't do him any good.

"I'm her uncle," he explained, "her mother's—Christy's—older brother, and I know you have her."

"I can neither confirm nor deny your allegations, Mr. Kraynick. Please call social services." She rattled off the number.

"Wait!" he said, unable to hide his urgency. "Please," he said more calmly. "Just hear me out."

"How did you find me?"

"A friend of Christy's."

"I'm sorry I can't help you, Mr. Kraynick," she said softly. "This conversation is over."

"I grew up in foster care," he said, as though that gave him some special privilege. Some insider's edge.

"Then you know you shouldn't be calling me at all."

"Yes… But Carrie is my niece," he said. "I need to see her. To know that she's okay."

"You'll have to go through social services to arrange that."

"I'm sure you know it's not as easy as it sounds. I'm a single man with no real ties and I've no intention of petitioning for custody. They aren't real eager to give me the time of day. I never even knew Carrie's mother. For all intents and purposes, our mother didn't raise either one of us. All I have going for me is half a set of genes. My lawyer's on it, but it could be weeks—months—before this is sorted out. Carrie could be adopted by then. Which would be fine, great for her, but then I'd have lost my chance. I don't want to take her. I won't hurt her. I just have to see her."

"I'm sorry, Mr. Kraynick, but…"

* * * * *

*Find out if Rick Kraynick will ever have a chance to meet his niece.*
*Look for A DAUGHTER'S TRUST*
*by Tara Taylor Quinn,*
*available in September 2009.*